THE BLOODY TRACKS OF

BIGFOOT

DAVID IRONS

SEVERED PRESS
HOBART TASMANIA

THE BLOODY TRACKS OF BIGFOOT

CHAPTER 1

Onion Mountain – Portland, Oregon, November 13th, 1980.

Winter held its corpse-cold grip on Oregon. The trees of Onion Mountain were shedding their brown leaves to reveal branches that looked as withered and spindly as skeletal arms. Everything was silent; then, an almighty scream tore across the soundtrack.

'Whhhaaaaaaagh!' Jack Wasson cried. His voice echoed out and up the mountain. His foot was tangled in a clump of brambles so thick and sharp his ankle was nearly severed. Losing balance, he hit the deck face first with a dull thud. His Winchester 1894 was thrown to one side; his backpack filled with camping gear weighed him down like a rock. He was laid out in wet leaves and mud, eyes blurred and jaw aching from the awkward fall. With a low, pained groan, he gained focus and pulled a dirty smile for the one thing that hadn't been upended – the most important thing of his impromptu hunting expedition: the half-full bottle of Kentucky Rye he had been swallowing all day.

Jack laughed now, ignoring the feeling of barbs and blood the brambles had left in his thick winter socks. He pulled himself into a sitting position, unscrewed the whiskey's cap, and swallowed another burning mouthful.

He pulled the bottle from his lips with a pop of air and a satisfied, *'Aggghhhhhh!'*

Kentucky Rye, now there was a real painkiller.

Nothing mattered at that moment, apart from his two favorite things: his rifle and his booze. Could life get any better than this? No, it couldn't. But it could get a whole lot worse. In fact, everything in his life away from these woods was pretty abysmal at this moment in time.

Jack Wasson was a simple man – too simple for his own good at times. He worked for Pacific Gas and Electric, attending call-outs for faulty lines and cracked pipes. He was a glorified fix-it man, keeping all good bill-paying Californians' utilities up to spec. It was a good job; he was basically his own boss. He would call into head office, pick up a worksheet and spend the day rolling around the valley, going door-to-door dealing with people's problems. He had a nice clean van and a nice clean uniform and a very nice pay-packet to keep his wife Joy and his two kids Terri and Mark fed and watered with a roof over their head. Everything on the outside looked perfect; the American dream served up in a good upper-middle-class suburban neighborhood. Station wagons, barbeques, and kids that delivered newspapers on B.M.X. bikes.

Looks can be deceiving.

Not everything in Jack's life was clean and shined and perfect. There was a black spot – a very dirty spot – named Vikki Gere, who was about to melt his life down to volcanic slag.

It started with a regular call-out on a regular Tuesday morning. There was an instant ping of attraction when she answered the door to her swank apartment in the hills.

'Are you the guy? The guy to fix my plugged pipe?'

She was all flowing red hair and more curves than a racetrack.

'Y-yeah,' he mumbled. 'I'm the man for the job.'

All those curves and Jack with no brakes.

And indeed, he was the man for the job. His Pacific Gas and Electric van started parking outside her home three times a week, only between the hours of nine to five, though, the hours when her dear old bill-paying hubby was out at work.

It was all fun and games until his last visit to her door.

'I'm pregnant,' she had said. 'I'm pregnant, and it's your fault.'

He had gasped, tried to think of something to help get him out of the situation, then spoke anyway.

'So, what do you want me to do about it?'

'You put it in there. The least you can do is take some responsibility to get it out.'

'Hey, I ain't paying for no abortion. You know how much that cos–'

'Okay, Jack. I thought you'd say that. I'll just go ask your wife for the money.'

She had slammed the door, not answered it when he had hammered it down until the neighbors came out. He had sweated about it all day yesterday. Sat and waited like a man on death row for the phone to ring or the door to knock. There was no way he could just cough up the six hundred bucks to get her scraped out – not without Joy knowing. The pressure had got too much. Then when Friday night rolled around, he had packed his camping gear, grabbed his rifle, and headed for the hills – Onion Mountain, to be exact. As he pulled out of his neighborhood, Vikki was driving to his home.

'*Agh, fuck.* Gig's up,' he said to himself, pulling the bottle of Kentucky Rye from under the front seat, chugging a mouthful while hanging over the steering wheel.

He had left his work van parked up out of sight and decided to spend the weekend living off the land and out of a bottle. And what better way to let out all that aggression than blowing off some defenseless critter's head? Anything to get away from the new reality of his life: Terri and Mark were going to have a new brother or sister, all because he had gotten some redheaded floozy who wanted some afternoon delight el-preggo. Like the old saying goes, he was literally going to have a ginger-haired stepchild. What could he do? His booze-blurred mind laughed at him like a carny barker: Ya dips ya wick and ya takes ya chances!

He had risked it all right. And right now, Joy was probably screaming at the sky, cursing his name with every foul word she could think of. He could kiss that nice suburban house goodbye. It was back to living above a pizzeria and paying maintenance for three kids while he killed himself working every hour under the sun.

He pulled another big gulp from the whiskey, not feeling the cold ground seeping into his pants.

Maybe he could stay out here forever? Roughing it like some kind of mountain man. The booze wouldn't last that long; he only had two more bottles left until dry-city. He had made it three-quarters of the way up Onion Mountain, had tried to escape civilization by going way off track, entering denser woodland to try and distance himself from his demons.

Suddenly, the face of a ginger-haired kid with all of the charm of Alfred E. Neuman – The kid from *MAD Magazine* – popped in his skull and started speaking: 'Gee-whizz, Pop! Tell me the story of how ya met mom again?' it bleated.

'I went round to fix her gas pipe, and the next thing I knew–'

'Then ya had me!' The imaginary kid honked out a laugh.

Jack took another gulp of the whiskey. Wishing Vikki's gas pipe was the only pipe he would have plugged.

His brain sloshed in his skull with the booze. Kids. If there was one thing he didn't need right now, it was another kid, especially one that wasn't Joy's.

'What a mess,' he moaned.

A deep crack came from the shadowed woods in front of him.

Was there someone else up here? It sounded like a heavy footstep …

A filthy grin grew on his face. Maybe he had just found dinner. Or something he could take his aggression out on, something small and furry that would pop when he plugged it with a slug. He wiped his eyes, screwed the cap back on the whiskey, and reached for his rifle.

That's when he saw them.

A cold shiver sobered him immediately. He couldn't have been that drunk to be seeing … what he thought he was seeing.

He wiped his eyes again.

He *was* seeing them.

The creatures in front of him didn't disappear, but Jack's grip on reality did.

What he was looking at was something from some dime-store pulp paperback, a bad T.V. movie, or from the front pages of *The Weekly World News*. He understood what had crept up on him while he was sprawled out on the ground. He was no anthropology student, but had read all of the names associated with them: Sasquatch, Yeti … Bigfoot.

There were two of them slowly creeping towards him quizzically through the huge tree trunks. They were all thick matted black hair and leathery skin; recessed boneless noses; protruding foreheads; gnarled fingers with claw-like nails. They looked like things that had crawled from the pit, but there was a gentleness to them, a feeling that they meant no harm. Jack blinked, understanding that it wasn't his lack of depth perception that made them a different height. The one furthest away was the taller of the two – a true Bigfoot – standing well over seven feet tall, and the closer, maybe about four feet.

'Littlefoot,' Jack whispered to himself.

Then, staring into their eyes – the windows of the soul – he understood their relationship: Mother and son. The big one was female, her deep brown eyes held this truth, and the smaller one was her son. A perverse smile spread over Jack's face. The smaller Bigfoot matched Jack's expression with a maw filled with small sharp teeth. Then a drunken connection was made in Jack's mind: This furry, leather-faced child was one and the same as the ginger-haired child that taunted him in his mind's eye. It was as devilish and unwanted as the one that Vikki had incubating in her – the one he was supposed to pay six hundred bucks to send on a one-way trip down the sewers. Jack reached for his rifle – if only all his problems in life could be as simple as reaching for a rifle – and planted its butt in his shoulder, taking aim.

The dumb little creature still came closer, unaware of the high-powered weapon he had pointed straight at the middle of its face. He wouldn't be living above a pizzeria if he bagged these two. He could have money and fame and all the easy redheads he wanted if he popped these two.

A putrid smell hit the air; it was like a wet dog mixed with a decomposing corpse. That's one thing the good old *Weekly World News* never mentioned, how much these bastards stunk!

'Come on,' Jack whispered, cocking the rifle. He stepped back slowly, the distance giving him the advantage when he swung round to plug the mom. The smaller one let out a growl that could have been a giggle.

'That's it, come to dadd–'

Jack backed into something big, thick, and hairy. That grotesque stink grew heavier as rancid breath huffed down on him. He had forgotten one thing, had judged this situation like his own. That when there was a mother and a son, there was always …

A deep growl vibrated out from behind him. It was every wild animal from every *National Geographic* documentary he had ever seen rolled into one.

There's always … a father.

Jack swung around and gazed up. There, towering over him, standing over eight feet tall, was the dad.

A squirt of piss fired down his pants leg.

This was the one that had started all the legends. Its barrel-shaped head held a rough evil face that stared down with eyes that almost glowed red with rage. It opened the black orifice it called a mouth; saber-like yellow teeth bared as tendrils of drool spilled like a pair of broken faucets out of either side of its cracked lips. It raised its hands that were as wide as shovels over its head, letting out a monstrous roar.

Fear made him drop the rifle. Jack understood then that this is what a real father did for his offspring: You looked after your own, no matter what. Then the creature brought down its mighty deathblows, crunching and snapping Jack's skull and neck, pulverizing the rest of his body into a pulp of gore and shattered bone. They were sounds that would have brought a smile to his wife's face.

CHAPTER 2

Onion Mountain – Portland, Oregon, April 2nd, 1981.

Spring had burnt away the iron-cold of winter; everything was turning green and balling up. Jack Wasson had never returned home. His family presumed he had run off, unable to face them because of the bun in the redhead's oven. The redhead presumed Jack had put a few more buns in ovens and had got out of dodge before the alimony kicked in. The one thing Joy and Vikki would have agreed on – if screaming wasn't their only form of communication – was when they stopped screwing him, their lawyers would. Life went on. And Jack's hidden van and the remains of his eaten corpse still hadn't been discovered.

A loud roaring came from the long dirt road leading up Onion Mountain, a plume of dust reaching up into the morning sun. Two identical GMC camper homes barreled forward like they owned the road. They were both cream with a brown stripe stretching all the way around, a little outdated for a camping trip, but perfect for the group of people they housed: a film crew making a low-budget independent slasher film.

Rob Lieberman – the director – was behind the wheel of the first camper. He looked like everything you would expect a hip, young, privileged L.A. filmmaker would look like in the early eighties: A Spielberg clone. He had the beard, had the sunglasses, and even had the baseball cap. The one thing Rob didn't have was the talent. This was the final day of shooting his magnum opus. A film he was not only directing but had also written, titled: *Mountaintop Madman Massacre*. His father, Big Bob Lieberman – of Lieberman's meatpacking industries – had fronted the cash and was credited as producer. He had convinced the old man – conned would be more apropos – with an article from *Variety* talking about how low-budget horror was the hot ticket for making quick cash. *Halloween, Friday the 13th, Phantasm, He Knows You're Alone, The Boogeyman, Maniac,* they were all prime examples of putting a little cash in and getting piles of cash out. The old man fell for it, hook, line and sinker. And after a weekend of thrashing out a script,

Mountaintop Madman Massacre was born into existence. It was the story of a lardy weirdo named Hubert Humphries that escapes the local loony bin he called home and wanders into the woods of Oregon to survive by picking off of vacationing campers. The production had run smoothly for the thirty-day shoot; everything was in the can except some pick-ups and one important scene: the big ending. A huge explosion was to be the finale of *Mountaintop Madman Massacre*. The surviving girl, Jenny, was to lure Hubert into a camper where the gas was rigged to explode. All of the principal actors were needed to portray their characters' corpses laid outside the camper as an offering of love towards the final girl. It seems during the movie old Hubert falls for the final girl's resourceful ways of escaping him and gets the hots, wanting to do what any self-respecting psycho would and get the old horizontal hustle on with her in the final act.

Behind Rob, drinking and laughing laid out on the camper's orange corduroy seats were his cast: the three guys, Larry Lerner, Ben Tramer, and Arnold Lebowitz; and the three girls, Connie Connors, Laura Somers, and his leading lady, Adrianne Heather Curtis. How he got Adrianne on the cast was nothing more than a miracle. She had been a child star back in the sixties, was a regular face in all the popular shows until she got her own show in the mid-seventies: *What's the fuss, Lucy Russ?* A heartwarming weekly half-hour about the teenaged Lucy Russ – the new girl in town – who must find her way in the world living with the kooky Aunt Roo. It was a ratings smash, and Adrianne Heather Curtis had become a household name. But two years ago, when the show was canceled, Adrianne Heather Curtis had become household infamous. Coke parties, all-night benders, D.U.Is.

One newspaper reported she had been laid more than carpet – and not by her husband! She was everything a rising starlet in La-La land was perceived to be by polite society: hot to trot, ready to go and with it and for it. But with this notoriety came a distinct lack of work. So, for a few grand extra than his other actors, Rob had got his film "A name." A name that was a little fried around the edges was no less a name than any other name, though. What did they always say? There was no such thing as bad publicity. The movie could make extra money from all those rubber necking cinemagoers that just wanted to see how washed-up or bloated she was. A ticket was a ticket. And as long as they were paid tickets, who the hell cared? In the camper behind them were the crew; Rob's cinematographer Danny McLaughlin, soundman Billy Zito, and makeup F.X. wizard Tommy Bottin. Tommy was featured in *Fangoria* and *Cinemafantasque* as the man who can deliver the blood and guts on a budget. He was a quiet man, an introvert in a way. Not what you would expect from someone responsible for some of the screen's most violent deaths. Beers were passed around; old tensions on set were finally dulling as the end was in sight.

Only one more day of living in each other's back pockets.

Only one more day until …

The real horror began tonight.

CHAPTER 3

'Finally! It's over!' Danny McLaughlin said, crushing a beer can and throwing his legs up onto the cushioned bench seat he was sitting on.

'Aw, come on!' Billy Zito replied, spooling a fresh reel of tape on his Marantz field recorder. 'This one ain't been that bad. Out of all this low-budget crap-ola we do, this one ain't that bad.'

Danny smiled, ran a hand through his curly black hair, and pulled a face as he mimicked deep contemplation. 'Yes, this one ain't so bad. Well compared to our other endeavors in highbrow cinema over the last year. Let's see, there was Blood Night.'

'Blood Beach,' Billy added, pointing his shotgun mic at Danny.

The two then bounced back and forth off of one another.

'Blood Frenzy.'

'Blood Bath.'

'Night of Bloody Terror.'

'Oh, Pit of Bloody Horror.'

'Don't forget Blood Stains at Cheerleading Camp,' Billy said with a wink.

'How could I ever forget that one.' Danny grinned.

'Tammy Tanner's pom-poms!' they both said in unison.

'What an actress!' Danny sighed.

'Yes, one of those actresses who puts all of her talents upfront,' Billy nodded.

'In a D-cup,' Danny nodded in reply.

'Seven films in one year,' Billy said.

Danny picked up a pillow lying next to him, slammed it over his face, and began to punch himself playfully in the head. 'Seven films in one year, and every one of 'em had blood in the title! Somebody shoot me, please!'

'No one can ever say Illumavision strays from the quality productions,' Billy added with a piss-taking grin. Illumavision was the small production house they had formed above an Italian restaurant on Sunset Strip. Danny did the filming; Billy did the sound recording, and together they had thrashed out two years' worth of commercials for soap powder and floor cleaner, only to move up into the world of cheapo horror flicks.

'Give it a rest, you two!' Tommy Bottin called up from the driver's seat. 'When did you become so proud you got all snooty over doing a horror movie?'

'Oh!' Danny exclaimed. 'Our driver speaks!'

'Your driver,' Tommy replied, 'would ask you to take over, but seeing how you've taken advantage of the situation and spent the entire trip here getting sozzled, I think it best you stay back there and keep drowning your sorrows.'

'My heart breaks for you, Tommy,' Danny said.

'Yeah, the big star has to do a little grunt work for a change, and he gets his panties all up in a bunch.' Billy gave Danny a nod to say he was only yanking Tommy's chain, but shades of genuine animosity were in Danny's face as he stared upfront to Tommy.

'Big star,' Tommy said with a roll of his eyes.

'It's true, Tommy old boy. You're a rock star of the new wave of splatter cinema. People don't want to know about the film you're working on – they want to know about you and your F.X. You're carving out your legacy one latex mask at a time.'

'You make it sound like I'm to blame for something, Danny,' Tommy said, reaching for the can of coke he had propped on the dash and took a sip.

'No, man, you're state-of-the-art. You found your niche – your way of making a name for yourself in the movie world, and for that, I applaud you.' There was something snide and sinister in Danny's words, a true feeling hidden behind his facetious demeanor. Tommy had a feeling what it was: That old film school snobbery that because he hadn't become the next Fellini or Bergman, anyone else who garnered attention was to be looked down on. Especially someone like Tommy, whose natural abilities and skill had gotten him where he was today. He hadn't had to drop a dime on education to be part of the film world; the film world had come after him. Tommy had put together a reel of F.X. he had made at home: Slit throats that pulsed blood; severed limbs that geysered gore; realistic heads that exploded like watermelons – *Scanners* style. And so impressive was that reel that the producers came knocking. That was two years ago, and now some of the major studios were catching onto his work, and after this gig, he was heading over to M.G.M., who were willing to dip a lion's paw into the low-budget horror market. What was a few million to M.G.M. to see if they could "do this horror thing"?

Not much.

But to Tommy, it was that big step up. He hadn't said anything to anyone about this opportunity. But Danny knew it was happening. That was the Hollywood way: Everyone else knew you had or hadn't got a job even before you did. Nothing had been said, but Tommy got the green light for the M.G.M. project twenty days into *Mountaintop Madman Massacre's* filming. On the twenty-first day, Danny's resentment had begun.

'Well,' Danny said, 'you can't be the whiz-kid at everything.' He leaned back on the bench seat, popped his legs up, and crossed them with a satisfied grin on his face. 'Looks like you struck out with our reformed star, the one and only Adrianne Heather Curtis.'

Billy stopped playing with his tape recorder and sniggered to himself.

'What are you two talking about now?' Tommy was glad he was facing forward; there was no way they could see the reddening of his cheeks.

'Playing dumb.' Billy smiled.

'Stick to the makeup, *sch-weet heart*!' Danny said, doing his best Bogart. 'Cause acting just ain't your thing!'

'I have no idea what you guys are talking about,' Tommy said flatly. But he did; he had plenty of ideas. The makeup F.X. king he may be, but a ladies' man … not so much. When it came to talking to women, his foot would always firmly plant in his mouth. A feeling like a growing bulge would expand in his throat, and somehow all the right words were lost on him. It was the same when he met Adrianne Heather Curtis. He had seen her on *What's the fuss, Lucy Russ?* and had found her kind of cute. But upon meeting her in the three dimensions of reality, his brain had gone gaga. Her brown hair and slender figure and full lips and those eyes … The list could go on like a scroll. In his mind's eye, in that sentimental part of himself that glowed with bright red romance, Adrianne Heather Curtis was the kind of girl he had always wanted to ride off into the sunset with. Too bad he didn't have the guts to tell her that. Too bad that he didn't take the opportunity to do something about it when she had told them that she was breaking up with her husband.

As if reading his mind, Danny said, 'Too bad Tony got there first.'

Tommy furrowed his brow. Tony Reynolds, the stunt coordinator responsible for the big explosion tonight, did indeed get there first, and the pair had become something of an item on set. If only he was as with it with the women as he was with fixing up a prosthetic.

'You can't be good at everything, Tommy, my boy. You can't be good at everything.'

Danny laughed behind him.

His smile turned to a lurid grin.

CHAPTER 4

Blondie's *Heart of Glass* crackled in and out of reception on the radio in the camper in front. Laughs came from the actors as Rob concentrated on navigating the winding roads up Onion Mountain.

'I can't believe it!' Connie Connors coughed as she took a huge gulp from a can of Coors, pulling a curly blonde strand of her hair that was caught to the ring pull. 'You outed Steve Friedman – *the Steve Friedman* – Hollywood producer ... for Tony, the stunt guy!'

Adrianne rolled her eyes, and took a sip of her own beer. 'I didn't out Steve for Tony ... Steve outed himself.'

Larry Lerner, the film's blonde hunk, took a pull on his cigarette. 'Honey, we know that you know that's the truth, but just wait until those tabloids hear about this.'

'Well, I'm hoping my other cast members won't be running to a pay-phone to cash my chips when we get back to civilization,' Adrianne replied.

'Don't worry about them,' Rob called back from the front. 'I'll keep the animals in line!'

'Hey! You're not our boss tomorrow, Rob. Our dealings end tonight!' Laura Somers said, brushing her black fringe from her eyes as she lit another cigarette. 'We're all free agents again; we can do what we want!' Laura threw a wink to Ben Tramer, the dark-haired hunk whose character in *Mountaintop Madman Massacre* was in a love rivalry with Larry Lerner's blonde hunk. Both of them had had a make-out scene with Adrianne – not the worst day at the office for either – but Ben had formed his own special relationship, shacking up with Laura on set. Both were free agents and in their mid-twenties without a care in the world; both had those perfect symmetrical features that regularly cast actors possessed. They could possibly make some attractive children in the future – not that their little fling would ever last that long. There was a unity that forms between everyone on a film set, a bubble placed around a production so that its reality exists within its own sphere. The outside world was the outside world. Eventually, your perception of reality was skewed to the confines of that bubble, and after it popped, going back to the world outside was a real kick to the head. Would Laura and Ben go the distance? Probably not. But it didn't matter. But because Adrianne Heather Curtis was, well, Adrianne Heather Curtis, even the most frivolous fling was headline-worthy.

'I don't get it?' Connie said. 'You could have had the pick of any of these bozos on set – even these two bozos.'

'We're open all-night,' Ben grinned like a goof.

'And real cheap!' Larry added.

'Jerks!' Laura said, throwing one of the camper's cushions at them.

'Thanks for the offer, guys!' Adrianne smirked, taking a drink from her beer can.

'Yeah, but – Tony?' Connie said, an expression that boarded on disgust flickering on her face.

Connie was none too subtly trying to say that Tony Reynolds was knocking on almost fifty-five. He wasn't exactly the usual Hollywood stud-muffin or beefcake that would hang from Adrianne's arm like a living, breathing accessory. His face was pitted, pocked, and marked from years of being a stuntman before he had become a stunt supervisor. He had a Southern drawl and acted as a refugee from an old cowboy film that had escaped from its celluloid frames. One day on set, when they were setting up a scene, Laura said to Connie: 'Hey, did you know it's International Women's Day tomorrow?'

Tony, being in earshot, let out a laugh. 'Don't worry, honey; we got the other three hundred and sixty-four. Whatever makes ya feel special.' He flicked one of the toothpicks he was always chewing at their feet and walked away with a wide grin on his face, muttering, *'Jeezus Christ ... feminists ...'*

What was it with these starlets? They couldn't see the woods through the trees when it came to men. Maybe it was some kind of daddy issue why Adrianne had shacked up with him on set? He looked old enough to be her father but came off more like her creepy uncle that was never invited to Thanksgiving. This question perplexed Connie, who had mulled it over in her mind since their first pairing on set. Now, after a few beers, knowing it was the last day of the shoot, why not try and crowbar the truth out of her?

'So?' Connie asked again. 'Why Tony? Tell me.'

Adrianne sipped from her beer, and sat back into the bench seat's upholstery, so she was nearly swallowed by the plush cushions. It became like a cocoon around her – a safe space to say the answer to Connie's question.

'Between us,' she said trustingly, 'Steve didn't treat me well. I had to file an injunction to keep him more than sixty feet away from me. Let's just after it didn't work out, he went a little … stalker on me.'

'What?' Ben asked.

'You all hear one side in the papers,' Adrianne said, 'but there are two sides to everything. He might seem like the all-grinning nice guy … but …'

'But?' Laura said.

Adrianne let out a long weary sigh. She scanned all of the faces that watched her while she spoke, trying to think of the words to articulate the situation with Steve. Then with reluctance, she understood how to save herself from reliving her past verbally: actions spoke louder than words. She hooked her right arm out of her denim jacket, slipped her oversized t-shirt off beneath. She bared her flesh from shoulder to elbow; thick-scarred lines ran down its length.

'*Jesus!*' Larry exclaimed.

'Oh my god,' Connie gasped.

'Like I say,' Adrianne said, quickly pulling her clothes back on. 'There are two sides to every story.'

The rest of the actors stayed silent. Rob's eyes were fixed in the rearview, watching.

'Right now, there's one thing I need in my life, and that's safety. And you can't get safer than a stuntman.'

'I get it,' Connie said, nodding.

This whole conversation was the first pin of reality that had moved in to pop their bubble. Then, the fantasy of the film world rolled back in like a boulder. The screen door separating the rear of the camper was yanked open, and a huge lumbering form was revealed.

'It's risen from its tomb,' Laura said with a flash of her eyes.

Arnold Lebowitz – the actor, playing *Mountaintop Madman Massacre's* overweight psycho Hubert Humphries – flopped down beside them in an old t-shirt and love-heart covered boxer shorts.

'What were you guys yappin' about? I was trying to catch some Z's.'

'Never mind,' Connie said.

Ben passed Arnold a beer. He immediately yanked its ring pull and shotgunned the entire can. He let out a satisfied sigh, then reached down the back of one of the bench seat cushions and fished out a lone chocolate Ring-a-Ding doughnut.

'Hey! I forgot about you!' he said and swallowed it whole.

'Gross,' Connie said dully.

'Don't put the man down. Old Arnie's committed to his work,' Ben said, slapping the larger man's stomach lightly.

'Being an overweight psychopath who enjoys human flesh is hard work,' Arnold grinned.

'That's right,' Ben added. 'Did you ever see Bergman's actors go to such lengths to portray a character in any of his cinematic smorgasbords?'

'No!' Arnold shook his head comically.

'Have you ever seen such intestinal fortitude portrayed by one of Fellini's actors?'

'Intestinal is right,' Connie sighed.

'No!' Arnold shook his head comically again.

Ben held his beer can to Arnold's lips like a microphone, put a finger to his ear as if a hidden earpiece were whispering to him, then spoke in a mock-British accent. 'So, here on the red carpet, after winning the Oscar for best newcomer, is there anything you would like to say, young Arnold?'

Arnold immediately belched into the can; the sound echoed around the small space.

Everyone laughed, the serious tension of Adrianne's story gone. Arnold was a big goof, but Connie was the only one who held a genuine repulsion for the big man. He was just so … *gross!* Arnold knew this and played on it. And below the surface, all the others did too and laughed harder at her disgusted face.

'Whooooaaaa!' Rob cried from up front. The camper slowly ground to a halt. A thin fog had begun to creep in out the front windows, and within it, a figure popped into existence.

CHAPTER 5

Tommy watched as red brake lights and a spray of dust came from the camper in front and jammed his foot to the floor. The entire insides of the camper slid forward. Danny and Billy cried out:

'What are you doing!'

'Whoa!'

'They just stopped!' Tommy yelled. He shifted out of the driver's side window and saw the reason. It looked like … some kind of animal was in front of the first camper through the morning mists.

'What the hell?' Tommy said.

Ahead, Rob and his actors all squinted to try and make sense of what was coming towards them. It was over seven feet tall, four legs … then, slowly, they understood. A park ranger on horseback drew alongside them. The horse snorted a stream of hot air over the driver's side window, and then its rider in mirrored sunglasses and a Stetson gave three quick imperative knocks.

The actors all laughed awkwardly, the fear of the moment gone. Behind them, Tommy relayed the information to his two passengers.

'Park Ranger,' he said.

Danny and Billy came up front to inspect.

'Great,' Billy said, pushing his glasses up his nose. 'What's old Smokey Bear want?'

Ahead, Rob rolled down the window and gave the best smarmy grin he could. 'Hi! Didn't see you in all this fog!'

The ranger's face stayed the same – as gray as the sky above them – no other expression flicked over it. 'Maybe you would have seen me if you slowed down.'

Rob's expression fell, his mouth as round as the donut Arnold had devoured. His winning L.A. grin was going to fall on deaf ears with this man. 'Okay … sorry, didn't realize we were going that fas–'

'What are you doing up here in the mountains?' the ranger said. He eyeballed into the back of the camper, his reflective sunglasses only showing the actors' tense faces back to them as he did.

'We're here to film a movie–' Rob's words brought the ranger's attention snapping back to him.

'A movie? What kind of movie?'

Connie, who sat in a red miniskirt and bikini top, suddenly understood what kind of movie it looked like.

'It's *errrrrr* … a psychological thriller, a crime drama about–'

Arnold butted in, 'It's called *Mountaintop Madman Massacre.* You know, it's one of those sicko flicks where kids go into the woods and screw and some loony chops them into itty-bitty pieces.'

The ranger turned to stare at Arnold; his movement was as smooth and precise as a piece of machinery.

'Is that so?'

Arnold gagged on his words. 'Yeah, an … I play the loony.'

'Sure you do,' the ranger said.

Connie's eyes winced at Arnold. The next time he put his big fat foot in his big fat mouth, she hoped he'd swallow it.

'I've, *errr,* got the paperwork to say we'd be here,' Rob said, rummaging through the glove box. 'You know the logging company up ahead? The Craven Construction site? They leased us the land for today and tonight.' Rob found what he was looking for, a signed receipt and schedule from the company' owner, Matt Craven, confirming where they were going.

Rob passed the paperwork to the ranger, who lifted his sunglasses and began to read. Laura smiled as she watched his eyes scan from left to right as they moved down the page, his lips mouthing the words.

'That vehicle behind, are they with you?' the ranger growled.

'Yeah, we're together,' Rob said, adding, 'Oh, and our F.X. guy, he's coming up in a few hours. You'll know it's him as he has a blue truck.'

'What is it *exactly* you are filming up here?' the ranger asked.

'Just a few pick-up shots,' Rob said innocently. 'We need to film some extra F.X. shots to beef our film up with. So we have a chance to sell it to a distributor.'

'Yeah!' Arnold laughed. 'More blood and guts!'

Ben punched Arnold in the arm so hard a ripple passed across his fat frame.

The ranger sighed disapprovingly. 'Well, your paperwork is in order. Just don't go where you're not supposed to go. And no littering – you make a mess, you take it with you.'

'Sure,' Rob said.

The ranger eyed them all once more.

'Okay, go on.'

Rob started the engine, and popped the camper in gear. 'Thank you, Ranger …'

'Granger,' the ranger said. 'Ranger Granger.'

'Ranger Granger …' Rob reiterated, knowing all of the actors in the back were holding in honking laughs. He nodded, quickly pulled away, and within six feet of moving off, the entire camper erupted in laughter.

CHAPTER 6

Driving another hour up the old dirt road, they found the place they were looking for: the Craven Construction Site. A square hundred feet of firs had been cleared to make way for the project – the ground was as barren as if devastated with a scorched earth policy – there was nothing but dry mud filled with tire tracks all around them. To the furthest end was a small hut – the foreman's office, and next to that, a barn for storing tools and deforesting equipment. Both campers parked side-by-side at this end, and with whoops and hollers, everyone started getting organized for the pick-up shots they needed to film.

'Now, animals,' Rob called out. 'Tommy is going to start doing your makeup one by one. So stay close so we can call you in when we need you.'

'*Okkkaayyy,* Rob!' Laura groaned. 'We'll do as we're told!'

Sunlight started to break through the cold concrete sky. Rob grinned; the addition of a spurt of the sun would help match today's footage to what they already had in the can. The actors began to wander around and explored their new surroundings.

'Come on, guys,' Laura said. 'Let's go check out that barn!'

Rob quickly reminded them, 'No accidents – *pleeeasseee!* We've got by on the seat of our pants so far, so let's just get this shot and go home!'

'Sure, Rob. Anything you say!' Connie said. She grabbed Larry's hand and led him up the ladder attached to the back of the camper they came here in. There were two rolled towels under her arm.

'What are we going to do up here?' Larry asked.

'Sun's coming up; we're going to catch some rays while we wait for Tommy to call us down.'

'Sounds boring,' Larry replied. 'I want to go explore around here with the others.'

'Fine,' Connie said. 'I'll just put my own suntan lotion on then.'

She sultrily swayed up the camper's ladder so Larry could soak up her curves. Not taking his eyes off Connie, Larry yelled, 'Rob! I'll be on top of the camper!'

Rob shook his head. Oh, what fun it is to be an actor on set. Being the director, writer and producer was nothing but headache city. While all the others could just frivolously forget about the production, there wasn't a moment spare when some aspect of *Mountaintop Madman Massacre* wasn't polluting Rob's mind. Adrianne wandered over to him: 'So what's the story, boss? How are we going to do this?'

Rob smiled; where the others always enjoyed the free ride of the production, Adrianne was always reporting for duty and ready to go like a real professional. Behind her, Tommy, Ben, and Danny had come over, all looking worse for wear with fatigue.

'And here come the rest of my loyal troops,' Rob laughed.

'Sleep, Rob. You should try it sometime!' Danny yawned.

'Why can't you be like all the other creative people out there and sit around drinking coffee and smoking cigarettes all day and just pretend to be a filmmaker? Your ambition is interrupting my beauty sleep,' Billy added, pushing his glasses up his nose.

'With a face like yours, beauty sleep is about as important as a pimple on the ass,' Danny said.

'Hey!' Billy protested.

'There's a place for all of us in life, Billy,' Danny held his hands out to Adrianne. 'Some in front of the camera, and some like you, with a face fit for radio … in Alaska.'

'Don't worry, buddy,' Tommy said. 'I know a guy who's a whizz with prosthetics. I'm sure he could give you a hand.' Tommy tossed a bloody rubber hand to Billy.

'What is this?' Billy gasped as he grabbed it, jumping at the artificial appendage.

Adrianne let out a giggle at their tomfoolery.

'The Three Stooges return,' Rob said, shaking his head.

'All I'm saying,' Billy said, 'is why do you need us *all* up here? Tommy's gonna take an hour a piece on all their makeups. You won't need Danny or I during all that. Couldn't we have had the morning off?' He tossed the hand back to Tommy.

Rob ran a hand through his beard and sighed. 'Well, I hadn't told you this, but we might have a problem.'

'Oh no,' Adrianne said.

'Problem? What problem?' Tommy said.

'Well, my old man has been getting a little antsy about his investment in this production–'

'Holy shit. He pulled the plug, and we aren't getting paid,' Billy said.

'No, No!' Rob exclaimed.

'He pulled the plug, and we are getting paid?' Danny added.

'For the love of God, will you two knock it off!' Rob sighed. 'What I'm trying to say is while we've been out here shooting, my dad has been out wheeling and dealing with one of his clients – a lawyer for some Hollywood producers, and they've had meetings with a few distributors. And yesterday … Avco Embassy requested to screen a rough cut of the film. They've been buying up these horror movies, and they're really – *really,* interested!'

Adrianne let out a squeal and threw her arms around Rob. A hint of jealousy squirted through Tommy's face momentarily that Danny noticed and enjoyed.

'Am I gonna be a scream queen?' Adrianne giggled.

'Just like Jamie Lee if I can pull this off,' he replied.

'We're happy for you,' Danny said.

'Over the moon,' Billy added.

'Couldn't be happier,' Danny said.

'But we get the feeling–' Billy grinned.

'This means more work for us!' Danny exclaimed.

'I take that back, make it the Two Stooges,' Rob said.

'Tommy here is more like a Fake Shemp,' Danny said with a wink to Adrianne.

She nodded, having no idea what a Fake Shemp was.

'Look, guys,' Rob said. 'I need to get a healthy-looking workprint cut together as soon as possible to screen. If you could just go out in the woods today and maybe if, say … Danny, you shoot a reel of second unit stuff while we get ready here: slow pans of the horizon; the top of the mountain; the sun filtering through the trees, atmospheric stuff. And if you, Billy, could get a reel of sound F.X., I could use some wind; birds in the trees; feet walking in the woods, you know, something I can cut together. Guys, it would really help.'

There was a child-like pleading in Rob's face. His eyes suddenly had all the youth of someone on the fresh side of their twenties.

'Yeah, of course we can, and congratulations.' Danny smiled. 'Come on, soundman. Let's go get set up.' Danny and Billy began to walk back to the camper.

'How long you think it'll take to do Arnold and Laura?' Rob asked Tommy.

'What are we shooting? His hands or his face?' Tommy replied.

'Just his hands and over the shoulder; all P.O.V., nothing on his face, but we need Laura's slit throat again but this time gorier.'

'You know what Arnold's like; let's do it all at once and touch it up as we go. How does two hours tops sound?'

'Perfecto,' Rob said and then called to Danny and Billy. 'Be back in two hours – we'll be ready to shoot then.'

Danny turned around and saluted back to Rob.

'Do you know when Tony is going to get back here?' Adrianne asked.

Rob nudged her with his elbow. 'You mean old lover boy?'

Adrianne smiled shyly; Tommy tried to hold in his sigh.

'Tonight,' Rob replied. 'Around about six or seven – just before sundown.'

'So, do you need me for anything before then?'

'Nope, we just need to film your final scene – the big ka-blooey – and you are wrapped. Hang out and come back to the camper about six? Then we can do your makeup then.'

Rob nodded at Tommy, and Tommy nodded back.

'Cool,' Adrianne said, walking past Tommy and squeezing his arm.

'See you then, Tommy,' she said, throwing him a wink.

Another flush ran through Tommy's face: Did she know he secretly had feelings for her?

He remembered Cassie, his horror-loving friend from high school, what she would say when she saw him hanging out with Tammy Richards, the 'Oh so special' rich-bitch from Beverly Hills: 'Keep on dreamin', dreamboat.'

Keep on dreaming.

Arnold came waddling over, a shit-eating grin on his face and chocolate around his lips.

'Tommy, are you doing me first?' he said, scratching his crotch.

'Sure, Arnold,' Tommy sighed.
Yeah, keep on dreaming.

CHAPTER 7

Further up Onion Mountain, near its vast peak in a shrouded cave opening, the creatures all slept. At this height, there was peace and tranquility, matched only by the crisp, clear air that revitalized the lungs. It was a spot peaked enough that no human without a risk to their life would be able to find them. The bleak cave had become the last remaining vestibule of safety away from human life below. These three were the last of their kind. They had managed to live in hiding away from the rest of the world below. They would only travel out of their safe space when absolutely necessary: when their supply of food or wood for their fire was near gone.

The cave was a small space, not high enough for either adult to unfold fully to their great height; only their young could stand, and that privilege was shrinking day by day with his growth. There was a pungent and palpable smell to the creatures and their dwelling: rot, unwashed fur, and sodden filth flesh. The rough walls held many images scrawled by the elder – the child's father – carved with flint. Images of their enemies, the human man the creatures pronounced *'Herm,'* and the bear pronounced *'Beeja.'* There was little decoration to the cave, only the displayed bones of the creatures that had fallen to provide food: deer, possums, birds, and rabbits. But near the cave's back, in a cold spot they used to store fresh meat, the stripped body of Jack Wasson lay bloodied and naked. He was little more than a skeletal carcass now; all the tender pieces of flesh and organ had already been devoured. They never usually killed humans, but the elder had explained in his monosyllabic way the danger of the stick he had pointed at his young. He had experienced the stick before, had heard and felt its thunder crack in his direction. He knew the stick dealt with death – an inherited knowledge from his long-dead ancestors, and understood he must protect his family from it. Rage had overcome the elder, but Jack's pulverized body could still be used to feed on. Jack's backpack had been dragged back to the cave with his corpse, and its contents had been given to the young creature to amuse him. The blue sleeping bag that was rolled inside had been used to line the young creature's bed; the clothes rags to clean with; the compass and map were items the small creature had no understanding of with its limited intellect. But there was something in Jack's things that had become important. Jack had an old magazine, a copy of National Geographic that the small creature had thumbed through again and again. It was full of herms in surroundings he had never seen: huge bustling stone skyscrapers filled with more herms than he ever knew existed. There were spaces and places and creatures he had never seen, and all that color that somewhere was a reality. The world was more than just the tomb-like cave, their hidden existence with only the smell of burning flesh cooking over a crackling, popping fire. There was a claustrophobic shell placed over the young creature's world, imposed by the rule of his elder. There were often times of bared teeth from his elder as he pawed through the magazine, a fear that the elder would tear it from his grip and feed it to the flames of the fire. The child could tell his father disapproved of the images he stared into, but the softness of his mother kept the brutality his father could display away. In a way, his father was right. A spark of inspiration had been ignited in the child staring into these images. He knew not of man's hatred for him as his elder did; he hadn't experienced the thunder stick the way his ancestors had. All he knew was their few brief encounters with outsiders had ended in the way the owner of the magazine had ended. The young creature looked around at his sleeping elders: His mother and father embraced sleep and dreams. He crept to the opening of the cave, looked out into the distance where that other world of herms and color and more than the cold cave existed. Looking behind with fear that his movements had woken his elders, he could see they hadn't. Now was the time to change his reality. Now was the time to find the places that were spread out on the magazine's pages. Rolling the magazine in his hand, with the innocence and naivety of youth filling his mind, the young creature secretly left the cave.

CHAPTER 8

Laura and Ben wandered around the outside of the foreman's office, staring in through one of the windows at the calendar on the wall of a scantily clad blonde, a filing cabinet, and an old desk and chair. A Thermos, a typewriter, some paperwork, and a framed picture of another blonde – who was most definitely not the same one from the calendar – sat on the desk.

'Imagine this was your world,' Laura said. 'This little world, with these things around you eight hours a day.'

'Hey, a job's a job,' Ben replied.

'It's not my idea of a job,' Laura added.

'Beggars can't be choosers.'

'Well, I can pick. And I wouldn't pick to come here to work.'

'Tomorrow we're going to be out of a job when the film's over. It's back to humping my ass waiting tables. That is unless my agent can get me something.'

Laura nodded at this, knowing with a simple phone call her father would gratefully dip his hand in his pocket to keep his little girl in the green and away from any job she didn't want to do.

Ben, on the other hand, was the son of a farmer in Wisconsin. Not only did he disapprove of his boy coming to L.A. to hang around with a bunch of sun-baked weirdos, he especially didn't want his son hanging around with a bunch of sun-baked *actor* weirdos.

'They're all light in their loafers and soft in their heads,' his father had said when he told him his plan. 'You could stay here and help run the farm – have a future. But you'd rather just go and try and make a living on hopes and dreams.

Ben looked at his father, shrugged, and said, 'Isn't that what you're supposed to do in life?'

His father had just grunted. And with that grunt, no help had ever come when Ben tried to make those dreams come true. This was just another difference between him and Laura. Was their pairing just to be an on set fling? As production drew to a close, the answer to the question dawned on him more and more: Yes.

'Come on,' Ben said. 'Let's go check out the barn.'

They walked to the old barn. It was a poorly built shack put up to store the Craven Construction workers' tools. Its boards were scorn and rutted, looking years older due to the old timber they had used to erect it. They walked around its full perimeter, and Laura said, 'No windows.'

'Why would they? It was just a way anyone looking to steal something would use to get in.'

'Well, how are supposed to get inside?' Laura asked.

'We're not.'

'Surely there's a way? Come on, it will be fun!'

'Yeah, breaking into someone else's property will be fun.'

'Oh, Ben. You can be a real bore at times,' Laura said with an eye roll.

'I used to live on a farm. I know the rules.'

'What rules?'

'The rule you don't go screwing around with other people's stuff.'

'I want to see what's inside!' Laura whined.

Ben gave her a sideways look.

'What's in there that could interest you?'

'Privacy,' she said, reaching up to plant a kiss on his lips.

Ben walked to the front of the barn, where a huge chain was linked with a padlock to keep the doors shut. He heaved and pulled at the door's jamb until one of the boards popped off to give them enough room to fit through.

'What happened to the rules?' Laura asked.

'Screw the rules!' he grinned, helping her fit through the small gap into the darkness inside, getting a good squeeze of her ass that made her yelp. Ben slipped through after her. The barn's innards were dark and smelt of dampness. Only small beams of sunlight illuminated the space, seeping through the cracks in its boards. Eventually, their eyes adjusted to the gloom. A couple of flatbed Ford trucks sat in the corner; their hoods were popped, and Ben lifted one up.

'No batteries. No one is stealing these in a hurry.'

'Hey, look,' Laura said. 'There's a water trough in the corner. Do you think they have animals?'

Ben came over and inspected. 'Nah, they're just using it to cool down some of their cutting machinery.'

Laura looked around the space; smoky cobwebs as thick as sheets of fabric hung in each corner. There was a small ladder to one side leading up to an even gloomier crawl space.

Ben walked the walls, looking at all the chalk-lined tools that hung from nails and hooks on the walls: axes, hand saws, sledgehammers, reeled lengths of rope. It reminded him of his dad's barn. Why did the old man have to be pigheaded when it came to his career?

Yeah, right.

One small part in *Days of Our Lives* and the dead love interest in *Mountaintop Madman Massacre* – what kind of career was that?

More than some, he surmised.

His mother had tried to send him money to live off, but Ben had sent it back. He wanted to do this on his own, wanted to make it himself.

A hand gently came down on his shoulder, making Ben jump.

'Look at this, it kinda feels like a hammock.' Laura was laid out in the back of one of the flatbeds, seductively smiling at him. Its rear was covered with a tightly attached canvas, pulled tight to each of its four corners by rope looped through hooks on the bodywork.

'It does kinda look like a hammock.' He grinned.

'Why don't you come to try it out for yourself.'

What the hell? Even if their relationship would end when filming commenced, why not enjoy it while it lasted? He remembered one night out at a bar when a blonde was giving him the eye. The barman threw him a free bar and said, 'Why fuck tomorrow what you can fuck today? Go get it, kid.' It was philosophy at an almost Voltaire level when you were single and broke in L.A. Ben climbed in the back of the truck; the canvas became taught. They started to make out, Ben's hands investigating her body as much as hers investigated his. Their movements became faster and more frenzied, the privacy of the barn the perfect place for the act they were about to perform.

Their lips unclasped, and Laura stared into Ben's eyes. 'Is the big strong jungle man going to fix Jane?' she asked.

'Yeah, just let me take off my loincloth.'

She let out a frothy dirty laugh, and as her mouth opened, something dropped from the ceiling and landed straight at the back of her throat. Laura's eyes bulged with shock and horror as the intruder in her mouth began to squirm and writhe, causing her to gag.

'What the–' was all Ben could say as she shot up, pushed him to one side, and coughed up the thing in her throat in a pool of sicky saliva between her legs. In the pool of bile, a huge spider tried to escape the stickiness.

Laura screamed, started to gag at the eight-legged fiend that had invaded her mouth, and then looked up. The barn's roof was alive with arachnids. Spiders of all sizes ran over the thick webbing above them, stirred by the reverberating wail coming from Laura.

'Oh shit!' Ben said, looking up and rolling off the truck.

Laura went to bolt as more spiders fell down attached to silky strands, hanging all around her as if trying to pen her in. With speed, she dodged around them and headed for the gap in the door. Ben did the same, shaking his hair constantly to make sure none of the small creatures had nested there. Both of them ran screaming from the barn. A new knowledge that rules shouldn't be broken set in their bones.

CHAPTER 9

Ben and Laura's screams rose Larry and Connie from sunbathing on the camper's roof. The sunglasses Connie was wearing dropped down, leaving her completely naked. Larry grabbed his shorts and began to yank them on. 'I knew going in the buff was a bad idea! Especially with these clowns!'

They watched as Ben and Laura brushed themselves all over, trying to dislodge any of the small arachnids that had hitched a ride.

'Spiders!' Laura yelled. *'The barn's full of spiders!'*

Connie and Larry began to laugh.

'Typical townies! They come out to the boonies and upset the natives,' Connie grinned.

'Looks like the natives upset them,' Larry chuckled.

Rob stepped out the camper they were on top of – pages of storyboards in his hands – and raised his dark sunglasses: 'What the heck was that?' he said.

Connie leaned over the side of the camper topless, her boobs swinging down to greet Rob, whose jaw hit the floor. 'The young lovers did a bit of breaking and entering in the old barn!' she exclaimed and popped back out of sight. Mesmerized momentarily, Rob found his bearings and stormed around the other side of the camper.

'What the hell are you goofballs doing?' he exclaimed.

Laura and Ben had finally stopped searching their bodies for spiders and stared at Rob, disheveled and speechless.

'Oh,' Connie said.

'We were–' Ben butted in but was quickly cut off by Rob.

'Were in the barn?' Rob frowned, looking over her shoulder at the popped board in the barn's door.

'Well … yeah,' Ben replied.

'I told you all to be careful around here. We got this place for a steal to shoot in, and if we lose it, we're up the creek without a paddle. If the guy I rented this place from turns up and sees you broke into his barn, he'll lose his goddamn mind.'

Laura looked at the floor like a told-off child.

'Look, it's my fault. I should have known better, Rob,' Ben said. 'I'll fix the door okay, we got a tool kit in the camper.'

'Yeah, just make sure you do, okay, guys.'

Rob walked off, putting his sunglasses on as he went.

'That guy can be a real jerk!' Laura said.

'I think we've been the real jerks,' Ben replied.

This was the fundamental difference between the pair: Ben understood what responsibility was; Laura didn't. In a way, Laura was privileged enough not to let responsibility even be a blip on her radar. If Ben had no responsibility in his life, he would be out on the street, panhandling on a corner like a no-good bum. Even though his father had no interest in his life, he had instilled a work ethic in him and some sort of moral code. The same couldn't be said as Laura flipped Rob off as he walked away.

Yes. Their little onset romance was most definitely coming to an end.

Connie saw the look on Ben's face as she peeked over the camper's edge and then rolled on her back. 'Looks like there is a little trouble in paradise below us.'

'*Awwww,* the love birds aren't singing the same song anymore?' Larry said.

'I think there's more chance of them whistling Dixie than being shacked up in a cage together,' Connie smirked.

'You know,' Larry said playfully, 'I don't think either of them understands the complexities of a true, loving relationship. The nuances and depths you have to connect with someone to realize they're your soul mate. There's a meaningfulness and trust most people wouldn't understand that goes with being someone's partner.'

Connie sat up and looked at him.

'You really feel that way?'

'Sure I do. That's what I tell my girlfriend back home all the time.'

They both giggled and began to kiss.

Below in the camper, Tommy had dressed Arnold in his bloody varsity jacket and slacks and was applying greasy makeup to his face for that "unwashed serial killer look."

They both looked up at the ceiling of the camper; pings and pops of the metal roof reverberated around them as Connie continued to laugh. 'Unbelievable, isn't it,' Arnold moaned as Tommy brushed fake blood to the side of his mouth. 'Everyone on this set seems to be getting laid like carpet, apart from you and me.'

Tommy sighed, missed his mark with his art brush, and smudged red over Arnold's hamster cheek.

'Stay still, Arnold.' Tommy grinned as politely as he could.

'It's true!' Arnold said. 'Ben's boffing Laura; Connie is boffing Ben, and Tony is boffing Adrianne!'

'That's not everyone, Arnold.'

'Well, sure it is. Remember when we shot the stuff at the bar with those three Playboy bunnies Rob hired for the stripper scene?'

Tommy wrinkled his nose, and added a little black to darken his blood mix. 'Yeah?'

'Boffed! All boffed! Billy, Danny, and Rob took them out when you went back to the hotel early.'

'Are you crazy, Arnold? Why is this the first I know about it?'

'They didn't want to tell you that ya missed out!'

'Where were you?' Tommy started to apply the fake blood around Arnold's lips again.

'At the bar, eating a pizza.'

'Figures,' Tommy sighed.

'So it's true! You and me are the same. We couldn't get ass if we were toilet seats!'

'Arnold, old buddy, we are *not* the same.'

Tommy looked out the camper window. Adrianne was pacing up and down where the barren ground ended, and the thick woods began. She was tugging her lip and seemed a million miles away in her eyes. Was she thinking about her performance for her last scene? Who knew? But Tommy smiled slightly as he stared at her. She looked absolutely marvelous.

'There's no point checking her out, Tommy. I've heard Tony's drilled her so hard she nearly ended up in China.'

Tommy threw his brush across the camper, staring at Arnold's big dumb childish face.

'Arnold, just shut up.'

CHAPTER 10

Danny and Billy had hiked an hour in one direction through the dense woods and had soon found their worn Nike sneakers weren't up for the rough terrain. The pair had done exactly what Rob had asked of them: Danny had shot any good angle he could get handheld with his 16mm Bolex; Billy had isolated and recorded as many nature sounds with the Marantz kit as possible.

'I'm beat,' Danny said. 'Come on, let's get heading back; we got what he wanted.'

Billy nodded, leaned against a great pine tree, and took the weight off his feet. 'Let's just take a minute. I forgot what life was like away from the goof troop back there. We've been cooped up with them for a month now. In a way, I'll be glad when tomorrow comes. Peace and quiet in my own bed.'

'You got that right,' Danny replied and sat on a rock opposite. The woods were eerily quiet; the further they had ventured up Onion Mountain, the lack of anything living had become more obvious. No birds hung in the sky and sang. And even Danny, the most inexperienced tracker, had noticed the lack of animal prints in the soil. Danny pulled some cigarettes from his top pocket and placed one between his lips, offering one to Billy, who shook his head. 'I get a kick out of the actors; Rob ain't a bad dude.' Danny lit his cigarette. 'But that Tommy grates me the wrong way.'

Billy let out a laugh. 'What the hell is it with you and Tommy? He's a good guy. He's done nothing wrong by us. I break his balls for a joke, but I know you – you mean it.'

Danny took a drag on his cigarette. 'He irks me.'

'He irks you. What the hell does that mean, Danny?' Billy slumped down the pine, planting his ass to rest on the ground.

'He's a creep. There's something not right about him.'

'Bullshit! He's just a kid! How old is he, twenty-three? Kid's been thrust in the spotlight with all these makeup F.X., and he's trying to keep his head above water. He just needs a little self-confidence, is all.'

'He's a creep,' Danny said.

'I've known you for fifteen years, right?'

'Right,' Danny nodded.

'I know you.'

'You do.'

'You're jealous.'

Danny almost choked on his cigarette. 'What, of that dweeb!'

'See, that clinched the deal. You're jealous! He's twenty-three, made a name for himself and going places, and we're still doing this crap.'

'Why the hell would I be jealous of all that … gimmick makeup crap.'

'Yeah, you keep digging that hole. If you got any more green with envy, you'd look like Lou Ferringo – if you know what I mean.'

'Oh, drop it,' Danny said. He drew in the final puffs of his cigarette, and nipped its burning end between his fingers. 'It's just … don't you want more from doing this film stuff? How many times have we met with execs, turned up with a spec script, storyboards, a plan, and had doors slammed shut in our faces?'

'Too many,' Danny nodded.

'I just want to make a mark. Do something that people will remember. Not just film crappy horror movies and commercials. You know he's going to work at M.G.M. Think of the door that will open there.'

'So … it is jealousy.' Billy grinned. 'Look, how about when we get back, we polish that screenplay we've been working on. Suck up to Tommy; if he's going to M.G.M. we could visit him on set, get out asses through the door and see who we can see, ya know.'

Danny smiled. 'Yeah, we could do that.'

'Being on this set cooped up makes you a little loopy after a while. See, I'm a glass half full, guy. You're a glass half empty. That's why we work together: We balance each other out. Come on, I need one final sound of feet walking; let's record them and get back.'

'Sure, buddy.'

Danny got up, reached out a hand, and pulled Billy to his feet.

'Okay,' Billy said, 'go over there behind that tree and creep out; any twigs in front of you, step on them for effect.'

'Sure, boss,' Danny said, getting in position.

Billy started the recording, put on his headphones, and held out the long shotgun mic towards the base of the tree Danny was behind and adjusted his levels.

'Okay … Action!'

Danny crept out, mimicking the movements of a prowler. His footsteps were soft but firm; a nice clear thud traveled through the shotgun mic.

'Nice!' Billy grinned. 'Now just walk in a circle around me from where you're standing, and I'll follow you, and each time you do a lap, go faster until you're running.'

Danny's face dropped. 'What are you trying to do, kill me?'

'Just do it; it'll sound great.'

Danny sighed and got himself in position as Billy tweaked the levels on the recorder, then gave the nod for his friend to start. Shaking out his arms and legs, Danny started to walk quickly, and with purpose, as Billy turned with him, the shotgun mic pointed at his feet. The sound of Danny's footsteps was crisp and clear as they traveled down the mic and up to Billy's headphones. Each footstep, pop of twig, and rock underfoot sounded perfect. Danny did a lap, and Billy followed him, the mic pointed like a wand. Danny's breath began to grow as his speed increased. It was a hard, heavy breath that wheezed, perfect for *Mountaintop Madman Massacre's* lumbering psycho Hubert Humphries. Danny's fast walk turned to a jog, Billy turned faster and faster on the spot, the sounds he was recording gathering a rhythm: Footsteps – footsteps – rock – twig – footsteps – twigs – twigs.

The sound wound round, spiraling over and over: Footsteps – footsteps – rock – twig – footsteps – twigs – twigs.

Danny picked up speed.

Then another sound entered the equation: Footsteps – footsteps – rock – twig – footsteps – twigs – twigs – *growl*.

Billy instantly froze and held the shotgun mic pointing off into the deep woods that stretched up Onion Mountain. What the hell was that? Billy squinted, adjusted the direction of the shotgun mic, and listened.

Danny slowed to a stop out of breath, a sweat forming on his face. 'Christ, Billy, you could have told me that you had stopped recordi–'

'*Shhhhhhhh!*' was Billy's reply.

'What do you mean, shhh–'

'*Quiet!*'

Tension filled the air; a chill shuddered through Danny. He didn't like the look of shock that held Billy in place one bit. Any heat that ran through his body dispersed immediately. *'What the hell is it?'* he whispered.

'There's something in those woods, something up the mountain.'

'*Something?*' Danny gasped. *'What the hell do you–*'

'I heard a growl. Distant, faint, but it was a growl.'

Danny crept over to where Billy stood statue-like and stared into the thicket of trees ahead of them. 'What the hell? It must have been a tree branch or som–'

'*Keep it down!*' Billy hissed.

Then the sound slinked up through the shotgun mic and into Billy's headphones, a throaty, hissing, growl: '*Grrrrraaagggghhhh ...*'

'That ain't no damn tree branch,' Billy whispered. His eyes grew behind his glasses; it was an expression Danny had seen once before on his friend's face when a washing machine burst into flames during a commercial shoot. Danny had laughed, saying Billy's face looked like a sea lion's pressed against a block of ice because he had gone so goggle-eyed, but he wasn't laughing now. A shared fear now engulfed them as much as plastic bags over their faces would. Billy pulled the headphone nearest to Danny away from his ear and held it to him.

'Just listen,' Billy whispered.

No sound came through the headphone. Billy's hand wavered as it held the shotgun mic as still as possible. The thudding of their hearts dominated the soundtrack. Then it happened again, only closer now: '*Grrrrraaagggghhhh ...*'

It was still distant, but it was there. The growl held a low gravelly menace to it, one that made them both slowly back up.

'*Christ!*' Danny exclaimed, 'What the hell is that? A bear?'

'I don't know, and I don't want to know,' Billy said.

'Let's get the hell out of here,' Danny replied, almost falling over himself as he dragged Billy backward. The pair swiftly crept away, gaining speed.

In the distance, the young creature moved towards them, keeping its distance not to be seen, and followed their scent back to the others.

CHAPTER 11

Danny and Billy made it back to the Craven Construction Site and leaned against the foreman's office to catch their breath. The pair had traveled back the hour walk to their campsite in less than forty minutes and were both exhausted.

'Try that thing in the woods; see if it followed us.' Danny pointed to the shotgun mic, and Billy quickly set up his equipment and listened into the woods: a gust of wind, a chirp of a bird, and the soft shimmers of leaves rustling on the trees. Billy sighed; there was no sound of … *the creature*. It was an odd word to use, but it was the right word.

'Anything?' Danny asked.

Billy shook his head. 'Nothing.'

A voice came from beside them: 'Rob's been looking for you.'

Adrianne walked around the foreman's cabin.

Danny held his heart in shock, Billy swung around and held the shotgun mic on her as if it were a weapon: both were pallid with fright.

'What's wrong with you two?'

'Don't ask,' Billy sighed.

'Do you know if there are bears in these woods?' Danny asked.

'Beats me. How would I know?' Adrianne said, eyeing the pair. 'What happened?'

The brush next to them shimmered, and something small and hairy walked out.

'Oh, Jesus!' Danny cried before he understood what it was.

'Is that your bear?' Adrianne laughed.

A small possum trundled towards them.

'Give me a break!' Billy cried.

'I'm out of here!' Danny said, waving a hand at the scene and walking back to the camper. Billy followed as Adrianne watched the possum wander back into the woods. Then, as she turned to walk away, the feeling of eyes on her made her turn back and stare into the thicket of trees. Deep in the foliage, hidden away, the young creature watched on.

A rough veiny hand holding a quivering butcher's knife moved closer to the cowering girl. Her eyes were wide, almost popping from her sockets as the blade was brought to her throat.

'No! Please! No!' she begged, but the killer wouldn't listen. There was one thing running through his mind: A thick schizophrenic blood frenzy. The killer let out a giggle from between his lips as he grabbed the girl's hair and yanked her head back, exposing her neck for the blade's deed.

Her final cry for mercy ended as the blade slit her throat and began sawing back and forth. It severed her sinewy vocal cords like cut piano wire, her screams turning to gurgling dull moans.

'Perfect! Keep cutting!' Rob yelled as Danny slowly zoomed into the gaping wound. Arnold pretended to drive the blade further into Laura's neck, as from behind the back of the tree she was slumped against, Tommy pumped more fake blood through a tube connected to the prosthetic. A syrupy spurt of blood jetted towards the camera lens. Everyone laughed as Danny recoiled.

'Okay,' Rob chuckled. *'Cut!'*

Behind the camera, the rest of the actors clapped and whooped. Billy's boom mic bobbed down and nearly hit Laura on the head.

'This feels so gross!' she cried as the corn syrup blood stuck her clothes to her skin.

'You have to stay like that,' Rob said, 'for continuity for tonight's final scene.'

'Oh, great,' Laura said as Arnold helped her to her feet.

'It was a pleasure killing you, my darling,' Arnold grinned, kissing her sticky hand. 'You were good, but I've had better.' He raised the prop knife up and down playfully, mimicking the strings of *Psycho.*

'Jerk!' Laura said playfully, slapping Arnold's arm.

'Right,' Rob said, 'we need some extra shots of Connie's death spasms from her hanging.'

Tommy pointed over his shoulder, 'She's all ready to go.'

Connie was already hanging from a tree branch by a concealed harness, covered in blood with a prop noose around her neck. She held a hand up and gave Rob a wave. 'All ready to go, Captain!'

'Cool!' Rob exclaimed.

'And no shooting up my skirt while I'm at this venerable angle.'

'Don't worry,' Danny yelled, 'we haven't got a lens wide enough to get *that thing* all in frame.'

Connie grinned sarcastically and gave him the finger.

'Hey, Tommy,' Rob said. 'Are the rest of these guys' makeup ready to shoot?'

'Sure are, all except Adrianne.'

'Well, we'll shoot Connie, so go get her fixed, Adrianne.'

'Y-yeah, sure,' Tommy said.

Danny gave Billy a look, a roulette of quick quips barreled through his mind of how to tease Tommy. Billy's look back shot the idea stone cold dead.

'Hey, Adrianne,' Rob called to her. 'Can you go with Tommy and get fixed up?'

'Sure,' she said, walking back to Tommy and linking her arm around his. Tommy shuddered at her touch, tried to play it cool like he hadn't, even though she'd noticed, and squeezed harder. 'So, what do you want me to do?'

'It's just the makeup for the final scene. You're going to have to get bloody I'm afraid.'

'What else is new on this shoot. Come on, let's get this done.'

Adrianne strode off confidently, almost dragging Tommy before he found his feet.

Back in the camper he'd drove up in, Tommy had set up a makeup chair that Adrianne now sat in. She was already changed into her final outfit: ripped jeans and torn denim jacket from fighting off the crazed Hubert Humphries. The clothes were already covered in dirt and fake blood from previously shooting portions of the end scene. Tommy searched through the camper's drawers and cupboards, looking for something he couldn't seem to find. *'Where did I put them?'* he muttered.

'What have you lost?' Adrianne asked.

'Polaroids. The continuity snaps I took of you guys when I did your makeup before. Billy tidied up in here; I hope he didn't toss them by mistake.'

Adrianne looked about the camper at the sprawled beer cans and potato chip wrappers. 'I'd hate to see the place when it's untidy.'

'Got 'em!' Tommy grinned, plucking the Polaroids from the back of a drawer under the sink.

Tommy grabbed his makeup kit, the old wooden toolbox he called his 'Magic Kit,' and started to mix bright red fake blood.

'Can I ask you something, Tommy?'

'Sure,' Tommy said, never taking his eyes from his work.

'How come you never look at me?'

Tommy froze as if rigor mortis had set in. He pulled an awkward grimaced grin to himself and answered with a fake laugh, 'What? What are you talking about?'

'I'm talking about how you never look at me, Tommy. Like right now.'

He gazed at her and moved in front of her with his arms folded. 'There, I'm looking at you. Does that make you happy?'

'No,' Adrianne replied. She grinned confidently and raised her eyebrows, crossed her legs, and pointed at him with the toe of one of her scrunch boots like an accusation.

'All through this shoot, you've acted weird around me.'

'Acted weird? How?'

'Well, no weirder than normal – you have to admit you're a pretty strange guy with all this prosthetic stuff: corpses and slit throats and axe wounds.'

'You forgot burns and hangings,' Tommy nodded.

'How could I forget. Seriously, Tommy, why do you go so quiet around me?'

'You know pointing out someone is awkward is going to make them awkward – it's like a self-fulfilling prophecy.'

'I say it as I see it,' Adrianne shrugged.

'Well, maybe what you think is wrong.'

'How intriguing. Please continue,' she giggled.

What was he going to say next? He had been awkward around her, and he understood why – he liked her in "that way." But he also knew why he stopped himself from getting close to her. With all these feelings bubbling inside, he put down the pallet of blood he had just mixed, and the one thing that mattered came frothing from his mouth: the truth.

'I wanted to be a makeup F.X. man for years – ever since I was a kid. I used to watch all those old black and white monster movies with my kid sister, and I used to try and emulate the makeup from the films on her, and do you know what? I could. I found out I could do it; it was something I had a skill and talent in. Then when I went to high school, I got distracted. And if I'd got distracted enough, I would have forgotten about my dream – I know it.'

'Was this distraction female?' Adrianne asked inquisitively.

'Yeah, I wore my heart on my sleeve like a goof,' Tommy replied.

'Did she have a name?'

'Tammy Richards.'

Adrianne smiled and looked down at her lap.

He couldn't believe he just said that out loud, but a part of him had had enough of her having the upper hand as they spoke. He could feel a heat pulse through him that would normally jolt his words dead in their tracks, but he kept going; everything he kept inside was ready to come out.

'All it ever led to was trouble. I almost never attended my first interview for my first film because I was hanging out with Tammy, and she didn't want me to go. I would have just given all this up, and for what? Her to cheat on me with some douche bag from the football team.'

'Oh, he's a man scorned,' Adrianne said.

'No, I'm just a man who's smart. I couldn't just give up on everything for someone else. I'm doing exactly what I've always wanted to do, and I'm doing well! I grabbed the brass ring, and I'm running with it.'

'I read an article about you. The youngest F.X. guy in the business and known as one of the best at makeup in Hollywood. So when are you going to allow yourself to be happy?' Adrianne asked.

'What?'

'You can't cut your feelings for someone off forever. Life can't always be about rubber ghouls and ghosts.'

'I just … I just have to protect myself from doing something stupid. I nearly did it once … and I need to make sure I don't do it again.'

Tommy shook his head. 'Why are we having this conversation? The last time I checked, you and old cowboy Tony seemed happily shacked up together. And by the way, aren't you still married?'

'You got me on that one,' Adrianne said. 'Look, being married wasn't for me – it ended up not being for my husband since he went psycho and I had to get a restraining order out against him.'

'I didn't know that,' Tommy said.

'Tony is … Tony. I need a strong man around for now; he's serving a purpose.'

'Who said true love died, huh?' Tommy said sarcastically.

'Yeah, so I fell off the horse, but I got back on again. It might not be the right horse, but it's something. Trust me, Tommy, you don't want to get too caught up in all this Hollywood crap and lose some sort of basis on reality. You end up doing things that … you never expected to do, just to keep a certain kind of lifestyle. And before you know it–'

'You become the front page of the *Weekly World News?*'

'Hey! I've been in some trash newspapers but never been that far yet!'

'Yeah, you need to get knocked up by space aliens or sea monsters to receive that honor.'

Adrianne laughed.

'So, why didn't it work with you and your ex … Steve?'

'Yeah, Steve. He wanted different things to me. I wanted stability and a partner; I wanted fun and freedom. He just wanted a stay-at-home slave that would pop out a kid.'

A shiver ran down Adrianne's spine. 'I honestly can't think of anything worse than being shacked up and tied down with a kid. I have my whole life in front of me! Why do I want to do that?'

'Well, I feel like we know each other a bit more,' Tommy said.

'Yeah,' Adrianne muttered. 'I'm sorry for being so presumptuous. I don't think you're odd for keeping yourself to yourself. I get it. Everyone should be happy, Tommy. Just don't cut yourself off from the possibility.'

Tommy smiled. 'Come on, let's do this makeup.' He grabbed the blood he had mixed and began working it with a thin brush.

'You know, we should go out for a drink sometime,' Adrianne said as Tommy worked.

'What is Tony going to do? Be your chaperone? Well, I guess he is nearly old enough to be your dad.'

'Stop!' Adrianne laughed, batting Tommy playfully. 'Can I ask you one more thing? What was your teen crush Tammy like?'

Before any thought was put into his answer, Tommy replied, 'Attractive, funny, and she had personality – just like you.'

They stopped and stared into each other's eyes.

A scream came from outside the camper's window. Tommy and Adrianne looked out to see Connie kicking down from the tree she was hung from as Arnold reached up with a stick to try and hitch up her skirt for a peek.

Arnold giggled like a child as Connie screamed, 'Get away from me, you fat perverted freak!'

Adrianne shook her head. 'Welcome to Hollywood, Tommy. Welcome to Hollywood.'

CHAPTER 12

The elder creature had awoken and found his young missing. It was an hour after the child had left the cave that the discovery was made. Instinctively, every morning, the elder would check on his mate and young, and without fail, they would be there. But today was different. The young creature's bedding was slept in, but he wasn't there. The elder searched around the cave, trying not to wake his mate, but found nothing. He looked around the cave's opening and up to the rocks above where his son would often climb, but there were no signs of him. Now the elder's searching became more frantic; he tore with speed and anger around their habitat, not caring of waking his mate, scanning over the same areas of the dark cave, again and again, coming to the same conclusion: he was gone.

Fiery anger lapped through his body, blistering his bones. The images in those pages that his young was so obsessed with – they had done this! The elder creature knew bringing in things from the humans would lead to trouble.

Anger turned to rage as the elder creature used his clawed fingers to shred the sleeping bag his young had lined his bed with.

Humans: no good had ever come to his kind because of them. He had let his guard down, folded at the whim of his mate, and brought human things into their dwelling. The sleeping bag was shredded to ribbons in seconds, and the aroma of the man he had killed and eaten – the man the sleeping bag belonged to – rose into the air, and the elder's rage turned white-hot. He let out a deep throaty bellow that echoed around the cave; it woke his mate and traveled out into the world down Onion Mountain. He would normally warn his family not to draw attention to themselves in such a way, but today things were different. He wanted his son back; he wanted things back to how they were with any influence of the humans gone.

The humans ...

A glissade of drool poured from his mouth as he rose to his full height and bared his sharp teeth with a hiss.

He prayed that any humans wouldn't come across his fury today.

He struck out and punched the cave wall. A crack blistered through the ancient rock.

Prey.

CHAPTER 13

For the entire day, the young creature had stayed hidden in the foliage and tree line around the Craven Construction Site and watched the humans work.

What were they doing, some kind of unknown human ritual? Nothing made sense to him.

The fat man in their group seemed to systematically slaughter each of them, while the one with hair on his face cheered him on. The young creature had watched the fat man go to work on one of his victims until the deed was done and life was sucked from them. Then, as if by some unseen sorcery, the dead had been resurrected! The young creature's face opened with wonder as not only did the dying human come back to life – they were even joyed it had happened! Laughing and hugging the others, while the one with hair on his face yelled '*Cut!*' Did their resurrection have something to do with the machine with the glass eye that whirred? Or did the long stick held by another human with its end covered in a furry animal pelt cast the magic needed to fix the dead into the living? The young creature didn't know, but his wonder kept him at bay as much as it held him captive to see more.

He understood his father would be awake now and searching for him, but he wanted to know more about the humans. When the time was right, he would join their group and see if he was accepted. He wanted to know more of the odd magic they used on one another, wanted to know more of the ritual they performed, and wanted to know what was inside the two huge metal machines that bought them here. There was food inside those machines, he had seen the humans come and go from them all day with things that smelt delicious. Even from this distance, their aroma drove his sensitive snout wild.

He would get into one of those machines.

He promised it to himself.

CHAPTER 14

Tony Reynolds tore along the same dirt track up to the Craven Construction Site as the two campers had earlier that day. A plume of dust rose from behind his old blue pickup. Deep in his belly, worry uncurled like a snake; it slithered up through his body in slimy ripples. The toothpick in his mouth rolled from side to side, winding around his tongue. Would he get away with this? He had to. He punched the steering wheel, looking down at his split, bloody knuckles. He never would have guessed such a milksop could put up a fight. Tony turned his neck to one side, ironing a kink out of his neck with an audible pop. Pressing his mirrored sunglasses up his nose, he let out a sigh that morphed to a growl. Goddammit, he *was* going to get away with this. He had jumped both feet into this situation, and he wasn't going to let anything get in his way. Those idiot actors wouldn't have a clue until it was over. He reached down between his legs and grabbed the Miller that sat trapped between them and had a long pull on the bottle. The beer soothed his nerves, drowned down that snake-like feeling that was incubating within.

'You can do this,' he whispered to himself.

A sadistic grin pulled over his lips, then split in two to reveal his teeth clenched so tight they could shatter. He had enjoyed what he had done tonight; it made him feel like a man. A man should stand up for himself; he should be able to fight for his survival.

'You had your chance,' Tony chuckled, wiping the blood from his knuckles.

Ahead, something appeared on the road.

The grin on Tony's face fell.

'What the hell?'

Tony's pickup began to slow, the dust clouds rising behind it dissipating to an orange mist. Someone was in the road, no, the road had been blocked, by… Tony's heart pumped so fast it almost jumped into his throat and gagged him. His first thought was: *Cops.* Coming closer, staring at the uniform, he understood who it was and said with contempt, 'Park Ranger.'

Tony drew the pickup to a stop, the engine ticking over dully. The road was blocked; Ranger Granger had got rid of his horse and had his patrol Jeep parked sideways, taking up the whole of the dirt road. Ranger Granger stood unphased and stared at Tony behind the wheel; the pair reflected one another in their mirrored glasses.

'What does this bastard want?' Tony growled as Ranger Granger slowly walked around to the driver's side window.

Tony took his hands from the steering wheel and tried to hide them, taking the Miller bottle and slipping it down between the two front seats.

'Hey there, Officer,' Tony said. 'Can I help you in any way?'

'Yeah,' Ranger Granger said. 'You with that film crew?'

'I sure am,' Tony said. 'I'm their stunt consultant and–' He thought quickly, straight of the cuff – 'and F.X. man. I have some props I need to get up to the set so we can get done and get out of your hair.'

'Hmmmmm,' Ranger Granger said. 'What kind of props?'

'Well,' Tony said, 'it's a horror film. It's all pretty grisly stuff, you know. Not for the faint hearted.' Tony tried to grin, tried to play it dumb, but could see from the Ranger's stony face he wasn't having any of it.

'Yeah, about that,' Ranger Granger said. 'I don't know if I'm buying into what you people are doing up here.'

'How so?' Tony asked.

'I met your friends up there today, and something didn't sit right with me. I have to take care of this mountain and its woodlands and wildlife; I need to make sure that you aren't going to be doing anything stupid up there that would put those things in danger – even yourselves.'

'You don't have to worry about that,' Tony grinned. 'It's all just a bit of harmless fun. We're just making one of those drive-in flicks, ya know. We won't be no trouble for you.'

Ranger Granger stared evenly at Tony; his expression was as unreadable as his own with his mirrored glasses on. Then, as if in reaction to their conversation, there was a loud hard metallic thump from beneath the canvas stretched over the pickup's rear. Tony's eyelids slowly shut.

Not now.

'What was that?' Ranger Granger said.

'What?'

'That noise from the back.'

'Noise? Oh, just some of the props settling in place, most probably. Look, Ranger, could I go? I'm behind schedule already and–'

Two more thumps came from the back.

'Let me see under the covering,' Ranger Granger said coldly.

Tony pulled a nervous smile. 'There ain't nothing back there but props, an–'

'I don't want to hear what you say. I want to see what's in the back of this truck.'

Tony sighed, staring out of the windshield at the cut-off road. 'It's 'gonna be like this then, huh?'

'Show me what's in the back of this truck. Now.' Ranger Granger grabbed the handle of Tony's truck and pulled open the door. Tony stayed silent for a moment, then replied, 'Okay.'

Slowly, Tony unfolded from the truck and walked to the back of the pickup. He undid one of the corners of the canvas covering and peeled it back. 'There, you see.'

Ranger Granger peered in. There were three five-gallon jugs filled with a brilliant crimson. 'Fake blood,' Tony said, pointing to it. Then, Tony reached in beneath the canvas and pulled out a rubber arm, the appendage molded to look like it was ripped off at the elbow. 'What's that old joke about giving the man a hand?' Tony joked as he waved the arm at Ranger Granger.

Ranger Granger whispered something that sounded like *'Sickos,'* then sneered to himself.

'See, it is what I said it is.' Tony smiled, was about to pull the canvas covering back when two distinct knocks came from beneath.

'What the hell you got under there?' Ranger Granger said, throwing Tony to one side and yanking the canvas back further. 'What the hell is this …'

Tony took the toothpick from his mouth and threw it to the floor; his mouth became tight and puckered.

'Explosives,' Ranger Granger said, reaching in and plucking out a canister marked nitrogen, then a remote control detonator. 'This is all pyrotechnics equipment. Are you planning on blowing something up?'

'No!' Tony said. 'That's for another shoot tomorrow. That's–'

'That's why you have two campers the same. One of them is a dummy car – you're going to blow it up in my woods!'

Tony had to admit, he was good.

Then another huge thud came from under the canvas.

'What the hell is that?' Ranger Granger cried, pulling the canvas back further to reveal a huge metal oblong: an army footlocker with a padlock attached.

'Have you sickos … got something *living* in there?'

'Nah, man. It must be something shifting around inside. It's my old lockbox from the army – I was in 'Nam, you know–'

'Open it,' Ranger Granger demanded.

'Well, I don't know if I've got the key or–'

Ranger Granger unclipped his gun and fed his index finger around the trigger. 'So help me, God, open the damn thing – NOW.'

Tony nodded. He had tried everything he could so the situation didn't go this way.

'Okay,' Tony said, reaching for his pocket and pulling his ring of keys free. He pulled a small silver key free and passed it to Ranger Granger. 'It's all yours, Chief.'

Ranger Granger took the key with his left hand, his right never coming away from the gun. 'Take ten steps back,' he ordered. Tony took ten paces back.

Ranger Granger leaned over the pickup's rear with the silver key and slid it into the lockbox's padlock.

'This some kind of special effect, too?'

He turned the key and threw the box's lid open.

Then he understood what was inside; his suspicions were right. Something was banging from inside the lockbox …

Ranger Granger went to say *'Oh my god!'* but faster than lightning, Tony was on him. Ranger Granger didn't stand a chance. Tony had been in 'Nam, and now that training of speed and agility had come into play as he quickly grabbed a tire iron from the truck's open back and leveled it across the bridge of Ranger Granger's nose. There was a tree branch snap, a burst of blood, a shatter of Ranger Granger's sunglasses as the impact was made. Instantly the man was downed, and Tony went to work, throwing Ranger Granger over his shoulders and carrying him back to his Jeep. In a flash, Tony had him in the driver's seat, slumped over the steering wheel, as he let off the handbrake and pushed the vehicle straight to the side of the road. There was no barrier or ditch to stop him, only the wooded hillside of Onion Mountain to barrel down. Ranger Granger was flat knocked out, unable to stop what was happening to him. Then just like that, the Jeep was off-road and sloping downwards.

'So long, shithead,' Tony said as the Jeep took off, flattening bushes and scrub weed as it gained momentum, the suspension causing it to bounce up and down violently. The Jeep became faster and faster until Ranger Granger stirred awake, just as it was too late. His dreary eyes understood what was before him; he was too slow to react even if he wanted to. A thick pine tree trunk was on him, coming faster and faster. With no time to react, Ranger Granger closed his eyes. The impact sounded like an atomic bomb going off, then the pain came as Ranger Granger burst through the windshield in a scintilla of broken glass and hurtled headfirst into the thick trunk. The last sounds he would ever hear were the shattering of glass and the snapping of his own neck as it broke in three places. As soon as it had come, the sound of the crash was gone, and Onion Mountain seeped back into silence. The road was clear now, and the roadblock had vanished like it had never been there to begin with. A thud and a muffled cry came from the insides of the footlocker. Tony grinned and looked in its direction, then spun the tire iron in his hand.

'One down, one to go,' he grinned.

CHAPTER 15

The day was almost gone; night had begun to blacken the sky. All the filming for the extra scenes was done, and the cast and crew of *Mountaintop Madman Massacre* had built a small fire adjacent to the two campers. They toasted marshmallows and huddled together like they were kids back at camp. Ben and Laura cuddled under a blanket together, as did Connie and Larry. Arnold sat by himself, too concerned about the three marshmallows he had roasting from a forked twig to be worried about female company. He really was a big kid at heart and wanted to goof around. Yes, Arnold could be annoying, but deep down, he was completely harmless. Billy, Tommy, and Danny all sat together, talking shop about film and effects and sound. Adrianne sat next to Rob, picking at a marshmallow that had lost all whiteness to the blistering heat. She gazed at the lapping flames, her eyes distant and fixed on a place and time other than where she existed. Every now and then, Tommy would hold his gaze on her a little too long. Danny noticed this but refrained from making his usual snide comments. Rob, unlike the rest of the group, was annoyed and agitated. The final shot of the camper exploding had yet to be filmed, and there had been no sign of Tony all day. He had said he had just needed to pick up the right explosives for the blast – 'I'm gonna give you a fireball with a sky full of smoke!' were his exact words. He had promised to be here at around four, and it was now pressing onto six.

'Did he mention anywhere else he was going to go?' Rob asked Adrianne.

She broke from her dream world, reengaged with the same question he had asked her fifteen minutes earlier.

'Erm … no. I know what you know.'

'Yeah,' he replied. 'I just need to get this final shot in the can.'

'I know, *Robbbbbb*.'

'Sorry, I'm a little antsy. I want to get the explosion filmed in case old Ranger Granger shows up snooping around.'

Danny, who was listening to their conversation, said, 'You do have a permit for the explosion? Right, Rob?'

Suddenly, all eyes turned to Rob. 'Yeah, of course ...' he babbled. 'I've got a permit to use the Craven Construction Site to film what I want.'

'Yeah, but have you got a permit to blow the hell out of one of those campers?'

Rob opened his mouth, but no words came.

'No pyro permit?' Tommy asked Rob.

No answer.

'Does the Fire Marshall know?'

No answer.

'So what's gonna stop us burning the whole woods down?' Connie added.

'We ain't gonna burn the woods down, are we?' Arnold said, drawn away from his marshmallows.

'We're not burning down the woods!' Rob exclaimed. 'Look, we made this film for nothing, and to do that, we have to cut corners. I spoke with Tony, and he assured me that he can handle this explosion himself. We can keep it small and controlled, and it can be safe.'

'What about if something goes wrong? You can't stop an accident from happening if there's no way to stop an accident, right?' Laura added.

'That's what the Fire Marshal is for!' Billy exclaimed.

'Hey, come on, I don't want to get crispy creamed from an explosion gone wrong!' Arnold cried.

A quick air of panic rushed through the group that Rob had to extinguish.

'Hold it! *Hold it!* Look, I hired Tony to handle this. You guys took on double duty today to fix Connie's hanging gag, right?'

The others nodded.

'Did it go wrong?'

They all shook their heads.

'Because we weren't careless! We knew the danger, and we made sure nothing happened! And that's what Tony is going to do. He assured me he had it under control and would be able to extinguish the flames. We all trust Tony, right?'

They all nodded.

'So do I, so trust me! We have one shot, we all know the dangers, and we know what to do to stop them!'

The sound of a truck rumbled behind them; Tony was finally here.

'Yes!' Rob exclaimed. 'Look, nothing can go wrong – trust me!'

Rob jumped up and took off after Tony.

Solemnly, Laura looked around at everyone's faces lit by the lapping flames of the fire and said, 'His famous last words.'

CHAPTER 16

'Hey, buddy! How's it going?' Rob beamed to Tony as he climbed from the pickup. Tony just nodded at him; no expression gleamed over his face; he was a blank slate.

'So … *errrrrr* … we good to go with the explosion? You got everything we need?'

'Yeah, sure do,' Tony replied, placing another toothpick between his teeth.

'Look, we, errrrr, might have a little problem with the others.'

'Problem?' Tony took off his sunglasses and slowly moved towards Rob.

'Yeah, because you took so long to get here – I mean, while we were waiting for you–'

A serpent's smile flickered across Tony's face at Rob's unease.

'What I mean is, they're all worried about the blast. They've been talking about Fire Marshalls and permits. They're questioning everything about this last shot.'

Tony snorted, 'Bunch of pussies.' Then asked, 'So what you tell 'em?'

'I told them you could handle it.'

'Goddamn right, I can.' Tony slammed the pickup's door shut and stormed past Rob.

Adrianne came running from the others and threw herself into Tony's arms. 'You okay, babe? Everything go okay with what we need for tonight?'

'It's just peachy, doll. I just need a little word with the other crew.' Tony shrugged her off and kept walking towards the group huddled around the fire.

'Hey!' he exclaimed, catching everyone's attention. 'I heard some of you ain't so happy with the final shot tonight.'

Any vocalization of their worry suddenly dissipated with Tony's arrival.

'Well? Cat got your tongues?'

Tommy took in a breath and slowly turned to look up at Tony. Adrianne drew beside Tony, her eyes projecting to not say anything. He acknowledged the look, and continued to speak anyway.

'We were just wondering if everything was going to be safe operating an effect like that on your own? You know, a single-man crew for a pyro.'

'You think I can't handle it, *Tommy?*'

'I never said I don't think you can. I just want to know what'll happen if it goes wrong? With no Fire Marshall, and–'

'Well,' Tony said evenly. 'There's your first problem right there: It won't go wrong.'

Danny turned to Tony. 'How can you be sure of that? With all these trees around and–'

Tony interrupted him, pointing to the small fire they were roasting marshmallows over. 'Look at that fire you have right there. Have you got that under control?'

No one said a word, then Connie piped in. 'Yeah.'

'What's to say that fire won't get out of control and burn the whole place down? The only way that would happen was if you are careless. Now, you're not calling me careless, are you?'

'We're not saying that we're-' Tommy replied and was cut off.

'Good, because I'm not gonna put anything at risk. Hey cameraman, you know what a forced perspective is?'

'Of course, I know,' Danny snapped.

'Good. That means two things – One: That education at *film school* hasn't gone to waste–'

Tony said, "Film school," as if he had just swallowed a bug.

'–And two: We park that camper right in the middle of this barren lot – same place you have your fire there – and we blow it. The explosion will be all filler, no killer. Thermals will pop out the windows and blow the glass, smoke will gush out, and it'll be a quick, fast burn. Perfect for film – perfect for that last shot. Old Arnold and the actors can be a good fifty feet away from it and not be hurt; the trees will be about fifty feet from it, and they won't be hurt. And when the flames dull down, because there's nothing around to burn ...'

Tony walked around to a space between the crew and punted a huge wad of dirt over the campfire, instantly extinguishing it.

'We just put it out.' Tony smiled. 'You pay a professional – and that's what you get.' He walked past Adrianne and squeezed her ass, making her jump.

'Now, I'm gonna go set up. If we want to get this done before dawn and get back into our own beds, I suggest you all do the same.'

Tony went to walk away, and Billy shouted over to Tony. 'Just to let you know, a Ranger is scouting around out there somewhere. If he gets wind of this, he'll shit-can all of us.'

Tony turned back to Billy with a grin. 'Don't worry about him.'

Tony walked back to Rob, who was still by the truck. 'Everything okay?'

'Yeah, I just straightened everything out.'

Tony pulled back the canvas covering from the rear of the pickup, and Rob peered in.

'You need a hand with any of this, let me know; I'll get some help for you.'

'Nah, man, it's good.' He patted the footlocker and grinned. 'I can handle this.'

CHAPTER 17

Tony was nothing but secretive as he set up the explosives in the camper. He struggled with the footlocker up and into the side door, grunting and swearing to himself as he went. The box barely fit through the door, and when Rob came over to ask if he wanted a hand, all Tony snapped was, 'You worry about doing your job, and I'll worry about doing mine.' So Rob did and blocked out the scene as Tony worked.

The camper was faced with its side doors towards the woods, which were – as promised – over fifty feet away from the woodlands to stop them from catching alight. They had already filmed the climax of Adrianne's character trapped in the camper's small closet. She'd picked out one of Hubert Humphries' eyes with a straightened coat hanger, then ran to the kitchenette where she turned on the gas and flung open a window, and jumped out. A point-of-view shot of the gas slowly creeping across the camper to a lit candle had been filmed, as had the shot of Hubert Humphries' reaction, as he understood that the camper was to explode. Now, all that was needed was the actual shot of the camper going sky-high.

Danny and Billy were standing way back, a good hundred feet away from the camper – just in case. The Bolex had a wide-angle telescopic lens on; the camper was framed so they could catch the blast perfectly. It was the big shot for the big finale that Rob wanted. The money shot that would put a bang into the production. Billy had his shotgun mic set up and working and listened through waves of static into the camper as Tony worked.

'You're gonna enjoy this old buddy … *Pzzzcchhhhhh* … that'll teach you a lesson you … *Pzzzcchhhhhh* …'

Billy winced as high-pitched feedback interfered with his snooping.

'He is one weird guy,' Billy said.

'You using the old glass to the wall technique, again?' Danny said, taking a pull from a cigarette.

'Yeah, but I can't hear anything good. Just Tony talking to himself.'

'Well, if all else fails in film, maybe we should start our own private eye service. You know, surveillance on cheating husbands and jilted lovers.' Danny passed the cigarette to Billy, who took a drag and passed it back.

'And a bullet to the side of the head if we got caught – No thank you!'

Danny laughed.

The night was cold on Onion Mountain, and Danny and Billy were wrapped in scarfs and gloves with no way of getting warm. This was the problem on film shoots: too much standing around waiting was a good way to get cold.

Rob went to poke his head around the camper's door, but as Tony heard it open, he flew over to hold it closed to a gap.

'I was just wondering how you're doing? Any idea when–'

'When it's ready, it'll be ready,' Tony said coldly.

Rob nodded, frustrated with his answer.

'I've thrown a couple of Norwegians in here.'

'What?' Tony gasped.

'Charges they use on demo-sites. That'll get things shaking. When the camper is rocking – don't come-a knocking.'

'Is this gonna be safe? I don't have to worry about any–'

'You'll get what you want,' Tony grinned. 'A sky full of smoke.'

Slowly, with his grin never slipping, Tony closed the door on Rob.

Tommy was touching up all the actors' makeup. They all stood lined up next to one another as he walked down the line with a pallet of different bloody reds that he applied to their various prosthetics. Arnold was officially wrapped now and sat on the steps of the crew's camper, watching everything with a Tootsie-Pop in his hand. Tommy made it down to Adrianne and began to touch up the bloody stains on her face.

'Do I really need a redo for a wide shot?' she asked.

'Hey, I'm not the director.' Tommy smiled.

'If you were, would you say I needed a redo?'

'If I was the director, I would most definitely think you needed a redo.'

'You would?'

'Yep. Especially if I was the makeup guy too.'

Tommy playfully flicked the end of her nose with the makeup brush and smiled.

'Hey!' she exclaimed.

'Tommy, old pal,' Ben said. 'Don't be flirting with the star, especially when her knight in shining denim is only fifty feet away.'

'Tommy's not flirting. We just have an understanding of one another, don't we, Tommy,' Adrianne grinned.

'The only understanding I have is if the guy in that camper hears any of this, I'd probably be tied up in there with the pyros. Anyway, I'm done.' Tommy finished a final dab on Adrianne and turned to Rob, who was nervously chewing his fingers. 'They're ready,' Tommy said with a thumbs-up.

Connie turned to Laura and said, 'Adrianne should go out with Tommy; he's cute.'

Connie turned to Ben and said, 'Get Tommy to make a move on Adrianne. What's he got to lose?'

Ben turned to Larry and said, 'The girls want to try and set Tommy and Adrianne up.'

Larry nodded, took in the information, and turned to Adrianne. 'Enquiring minds want to know, what're the chances of you sitting on Tommy's face before the night is over?'

Adrianne rolled her eyes.

Rob stepped towards them and began to do his job. 'Okay now – this is it! The last shot and we have one attempt at this, so let's get it right. I've marked out where fifty feet away from that blast will be, and I need you guys all laid out like we did before – when your corpses were Hubert Humphries' token of love to Adrianne's character. Only this time, Adrianne, you're going to run like hell from that window like you just jumped out a doorway to hell. You bolt straight through their bodies and keep going, but when you are level with them – BLAM! That's when we are going to blow that thing. And the most important thing is no one moves, or flinches, or reacts – you're all supposed to be dead. Any movement or reaction will be a dead giveaway that you're just playing dead and the shot's ruined. That's it. If it's unusable – we don't have an ending.'

'Jeez,' Connie moaned. 'Not too much pressure, Rob …'

'If I don't tell you how it is – how important this ending is to everything – how will you know?' There was a seriousness to Rob; the stress of dealing with Tony had got to him.

'Okay, we get it, man,' Ben said softly.

'No, I don't think you get it. All you have to do is one thing: don't move. When that thing goes up, it's going to go pop, and natural instinct is to jump or shudder – well, you can't!'

'We get it!' Connie exclaimed. 'Do you want us to get in position?'

Rob nodded. He was being an ass, but Tony had rattled him, and fear that a workprint wouldn't be ready for the producers' meeting was beginning to stir inside him. 'I'm sorry. I'm just under a lot of pressure.'

Connie nodded. She looked as if she might say something, but she didn't.

Adrianne walked up to Rob. 'You sure you're okay?'

'Yeah, let's get this done. Can you go stand next to the window you're supposed to jump through?'

'Sure, Rob,' she said with a dour grin.

All of the actors met at the fifty-foot mark Rob had made and got into position as corpses. As Connie lay there in the dirt on her side, she crossed her fingers, hoping playing a corpse wasn't a prophecy for becoming a real one.

CHAPTER 18

The two elder creatures had followed the scent of their young the whole day; they had gradually moved down Onion Mountain covertly through the thickets of trees. The female had managed to keep the male pacified – a rare thing with his volcanic temper. She had told him that they would find their young, that everything would be all right, even though, in truth, a burning worry ate through her body. As day became night, a new scent came to them, one that made the male's brow furrow and his lips curl to a quivering snarl: Humans. Their stench became stronger the further they traveled, and the more the aroma grew, as did the rage of the male. He straightened to his full height, his clawed fingers curling and uncurling as rage surged through his body. The scent of their young was mixed with the scent of the humans. If the humans had done anything to the young, he would …

'*No*,' the female mewed. They had to think of his safety, their safety; he wouldn't have gone near humans – you have taught him otherwise.

A spiteful tension shot through the male's body; a ripple burst over his black fur. His mate's words were true. But he couldn't help thinking of the book of human images they had taken from the man. Those images had stirred something in his son, an inquisitive nature that had bloomed to a fascination. As drool poured from the sides of his mouth, falling from between his sharp teeth, he wondered how far that fascination would go.

As they continued to travel, distant flickering flames and the smell of burning wood slinked through the forest. It was a camp – a human camp. The scent of their young had been here recently. The elder breathed out in a rough, throaty hiss. His instinct was to storm in as the aggressor, to take no mercy when it came to the humans. His mate stopped him, signaling that they split up, that they make their own way around the barren land where the humans had parked their metal vehicles. She would go one way, he would go the other. They would meet in the middle, hopefully with one of them with their young. The male agreed, grunted to warn his mate to stay silent and camouflaged, then they separated in opposite directions in the night.

Their young had watched the humans all day with fascination. This wasn't what he expected from them; nothing like this was depicted in the images he had studied. All of them were bruised and bloodied and told what to do by the one with fur on his face, then stared at the other two humans with the mechanical eye machine. He watched hidden in foliage as another man climbed from the back door of the huge camper van, brushing his hands as he smiled to himself and spat on the earth. Something about this man made the young creature wrinkle its nose and let out a wheezing growl. The noise caught the man's attention, and he stared straight to where the young creature hid. Then the man with fur on his face walked around the camper.

'Tony, how we doing, man?'

'Rob, quit being such a tight-ass. It's done, and we're ready to go.'

'I love you, Tony – I love ya!'

'Yeah – yeah. You got them all blocked out?'

'They're exactly where you marked out.'

'Good,' Tony said. He reached into his back pocket and pulled out a small black box, and extended a long silver telescopic antenna from it. 'It's all radio-controlled. All we have to do is flip this switch on the side, press the red button in the middle, and – Ka-blam! You got yourself a final shot, amigo.'

A grin curled over Rob's face.

Tony clapped him on the back. 'That's the first time I've seen you smile all day.'

Rob went to answer, but Tony cut in, 'Come on; let's blow this pop-stand to the moon. You can have the honors.' Tony handed Rob the radio detonator, clapped him on the back again, and led him to the other side of the camper, where the actors lay in position.

The small creature heard all of this and watched the two humans go. Then, with his animalistic instinct, he sensed something else. Something was in trouble; something nearby and hidden … there was … something in the camper … something imprisoned that wanted to be free. A feeling of what his elder had always told him that the humans were evil and devious lapped through his mind. Although he was carnivorous, he had always been taught not to prolong the death of the thing they killed. But the humans didn't even respect the life of their own! There was something in that camper, something hidden and bound that very much wanted to be released. The man who spat on the ground was responsible. The images he had studied and dreamed of in the magazine were false, and his father's words were true: There was nothing viler than the humans – he knew that now. He let out a growl again. Distantly he could hear the muffled cry of the captured creature. It was another human – yes, it was! It was inside the metal vehicle, unable to free itself. He understood what he had to do; he couldn't let whoever was in there be prey for these humans. Silently, he crept from the undergrowth, moved towards the camper's door, pulled it open, and moved inside. Just behind him in the forest, the creature's mother, who was circling the humans' camp, let out a whimper as she saw her young doing exactly what she had hoped he wouldn't be: interacting with the humans. Knowing the chaos this would cause with her mate, quickly she moved through the shadowy night and followed him inside.

Adrianne was in position outside the camper. She turned, hearing what sounded like movement inside. She looked around: all of the actors were outside, so were the crew.

Rob and Tony were just walking up to Danny, Tommy, and Billy.

'This is it,' Rob said, a nervous quiver in his voice, then cupped his hand and began to shout. 'Right, this is it! Everyone remember we have one shot at this–'

'Sure,' Connie uttered to herself.

'Guys on the floor, stay still! Adrianne, when I call action, run like hell, baby – run like hell!'

'Got it!' she shouted.

The female creature opened the camper door, sensing the humans were only on the other side of the metal wall. As soon as she entered, her son turned and let out a small welcoming growl.

His mother huffed and grunted in return, telling him to leave —
now!

Outside, Billy squinted his eyes as the sounds of the
creatures came through momentarily on his headphones.
    'We rolling?' Rob asked.
    'Yeah,' Danny said, firing the Bolex to a whirring life.
    'Billy?' Rob asked.
    'Sure,' Billy said, distracted.
    'Okay, I'm gonna count you in!' Rob shouted.

The elder male creature whipped around from the other side
of the Craven Construction Site. He peered through tree
branches that reached down like skeletal fingers and watched as
the humans bellowed to one another. A flush of fury washed
over his face. Who did they think they were, causing trouble on
his mountain?

'Five!' Rob yelled.
The small creature came over, yanked at his mother, trying to
coax her to what he had found inside the small wardrobe built
inside the camper.
    'Four!'
Billy winced. What the hell were those noises … was that …
the thing they heard in the woods earlier?
    'Three!'
Adrianne bounced on the spot, loosening herself up, trying
not to pay attention to the noises coming from the camper. *This
is it,'* she whispered to herself.
    'Two!'
The young creature's mother drew closer to the wardrobe,
looking in at her young's find. Her face dropped with surprise as
the thing inside's face opened in terror.
    'One!'
The female creature went against everything her mate had
lectured to them; her heart followed the same route as her
young's and reached down to help. The young creature cried in

happiness; he had done the right thing; his mother could see what he had found and understood why he had entered the human's domain! He let out a growl.

Adrianne's head turned upon hearing it.

Billy's eyes widened – it was the creature!

'Action!'

Slammed back into the moment, Adrianne took off, running at full speed towards the other actors all playing dead. She glanced at their faces tightened and expecting what was about to happen next. She launched over Connie, who she heard let out a gasp, as Tony screamed, 'Do it!'

Rob, grinning ear to ear, pressed the button.

All hell broke loose.

CHAPTER 19

Everything happened all at once, but each part played in suspenseful slow motion.

The camper exploded in a blinding blast that ripped through its insides as fast as snapped fingers. The might of the explosion was so intense the camper seemed to jump off the ground. Every panel creased and expanded from the inside out like a tin can placed on an open fire; its sides swelled as lapping orange flames blew out every window with a shower of glass; wafts of fire were spat out into the night air. The surrounding woodlands illuminated as if the sun had suddenly risen; spindly tree branches momentarily looked like cracks in the night sky. The sound was immense; each crew member reached up to shield his or her eyes and ears. The levels on Billy's Marantz recorder blew off the chart; every needle was buried as the sound amplified by the shotgun mic scrambled his brains.

A sudden gust of heat rushed over Adrianne's back as her feet pounded into the ground, real fear injecting through her veins as the idea she was about to be engulfed by flames made her run faster than she'd ever run before.

Connie, Larry, Laura, and Ben tensed up and squeezed their eyes shut as the ground beneath them vibrated. The inside of their lids turned orange from the intense blast of heat. Not one of them moved a muscle enough to be caught on camera. The words: *'I want to go home! I want to go home!'* ran through Connie's mind as silent tears spilled down the sides of her cheek. She was so concerned with stopping herself from jumping by the blast she hadn't considered the fact she was going to be just over fifty feet away from it as the camper went up. A trickle of piss shot down the inside of her leg.

Arnold, who was sitting on the steps of the other camper, fell flat on his ass, mouth agape in awe at the spectacle of the explosion. All of the flames that poured from the blown windows and doors connected around the camper, then wisped up to a mushroom cloud in the night sky. Tony was right; not a single flame had come near to the surrounding trees, but how the hell were they going to put it out?

Adrianne had run straight towards Rob and the others and fell into Tony's arms.

'Holy shit!' she cried, shaking, gasping for air.

Danny was still fixed to the eyepiece of the Bolex, mouth open in shock at the sight of the camper becoming a silhouette surrounded by burning orange.

'What the hell did you put in that thing?' Tommy cried, blinking away the burned-in image of the explosion from his retina.

'Everything it needed,' Tony grinned.

Adrianne pulled away from Tony and hugged Tommy. 'Did it look good?' she coughed.

Tommy was lost for words, shocked by the blast and taken back by the intense hug Adrianne had on him. 'It looked perfect,' was all he said.

Rob stood opened mouthed, staring at the carnage he had created. He wasn't in the Craven Construction Site on Onion Mountain at that moment; he was stuck in his own mind in someplace between celluloid and reality. Thinking about how the blast looked on film, how it would cut with the other footage they had in the can, and how he could end the movie with this one image of the burning camper.

'Are you going to call it or what!' Danny screamed, pulling away from the camera's eyepiece.

Rob went to talk but sounded like he was gargling with marbles. Then the words finally came. 'Yea – Yeah!'

'Well, do it!' Danny cried.

'Come on, get them out of there!' Tommy yelled.

'Rob!' Billy added.

Tony only grinned. A deep satisfaction of the blast he was responsible for.

Rob came out of his trance, got his bearings, and understood he was still a part of the world around him. 'Cut! Cut! Cut! *Cutttttt!'*

'Get out of there!' Tommy cried.

Re-animated by Rob's command, the actors on the ground struggled to their feet and ran towards the rest of the crew.

'What a rush!' Larry yelled.

'Far-fucking-out!' Laura cried, pirouetting on the spot.

'I want to go home!' Connie cried, falling into Billy. He dropped the shotgun mic and hugged her.

'How the hell are we gonna put that out?' Ben said.

'It'll burn out quick enough,' Tony said calmly, the blaze reflecting in the lenses of his mirrored glasses. 'I drained the gas tank and stashed it in the back of my truck, so there's no chance she will blow for real. When she stops generating heat, I've got some extinguishers to put her down.'

Arnold came running over; none of the others had seen him move so fast.

'Waaaa-hooooo!' he yelled.

Hidden opposite in the woodland, the hulking creature had backed away further into the shadows. The sight of humans celebrating made the cords on his neck tighten. Why had they come here to devastate his mountain in this way? His hatred of them exacerbated each second he spent staring at them. The flames pouring from the camper fueled the anger inside of him. Then, his huge chest hitched. Where were his mate and child? The question was about to be answered.

Rob turned to the cast and crew of *Mountaintop Madman Massacre,* grinned like he had never grinned before, and cried, 'And that, my friends, is a wrap!'

They all started to holler and cheer.

Billy let go of Connie, picked up the shotgun mic, and a new sound came through the roar of flame, one that made his eyes almost pop from his skull.

There had been a thudding and banging in the camper as it burned; none of them considered this out of the ordinary. Now, the real horror was about to begin.

CHAPTER 20

A pained primal scream cut through the roar of flames; the entire cast and crew turned in shocked awe to stare at the burning camper.

Billy jumped, and exclaimed, 'What the hell was tha–'

Then, the camper's side paneling started thumping rhythmically, pounded from the inside violently until a gaping hole was made where a sheet had come free. Something burst from the flames with an inhuman cry.

'Holy shit! There's someone in there!' Tommy screamed as the silhouetted figure leapt free from the flames and writhed on the ground.

Adrianne moved away from Tommy and fell into Tony's arms. For the first time in the entire shoot, Tony showed another emotion apart from arrogance: pure, undiluted shock.

'What have I done?' wheezed Rob. He fell to his knees, life visibly draining from his face as he stared as the figure dropped into the cold dirt and began to roll to put itself out.

'Get the extinguisher!' Tommy yelled, grabbing hold of Tony, who only gave him a fearful, frozen stare back. 'Fuck!' Tommy yelled, taking off towards Tony's truck.

The figure writhed and rolled and groaned, arms reaching up and flailing around, trying to escape the fire that engulfed it only to exacerbate the burn.

'What do we d?!' Connie screamed, her face a flood of tears and terror.

Tommy had pulled the canvas covering from the back of Tony's truck and was searching for whatever precaution he had brought to douse the camper's flames. All he could find was one measly fire extinguisher. It wasn't enough for the entire vehicle, but it was for the burning body that had escaped. He took off, pulling the pin from the red canister, and pointed the hose attached straight in front of him. He neared the figure; its movements were reduced to a shuddering death rattle, the smell of burning flesh and … fur filled his nostrils. He let rip with the extinguisher; a giant plume of white powder coughed all over the figure, instantly extinguishing it. Tommy coughed and choked as the extinguisher's powder entered his eyes and lungs. Instinctively he jerked backward, wheezing and spluttering, unable to see or breathe. The others all came running over, Connie still on the ground, a blubbering, jabbering mess.

'We gotta get them help,' Rob whimpered as the smoke and fire extinguisher powder settled. 'We gotta–'

Then the figure Tommy had put out came clear. Every one of the cast and crew's eyes widened. Whatever was on the floor before them moaned aberrantly, its tone wounded and crazed. It reached up towards them and, opening its arms from its bosom, a smaller figure it was holding fell free and rolled onto the ground next to it. Both of them moaned in dying breaths as the realization was made: Whatever they were, they weren't human.

CHAPTER 21

Connie's sobs became deeper as she grabbed desperately onto Larry. 'Are they … bears?' As the words fell from her mouth, they felt all wrong staring into the burnt visages of the creatures. They were all thick matted black hair – longer than any bears – and leathery skin. They had recessed boneless noses – no snouts – protruding humanoid foreheads. There were no paws, just rough hands with gnarled fingers and claw-like nails. It was easy to distinguish, one was female, and one was male. All the appropriate genitalia were there under nubs of burnt fur. It was a mother and her son.

'What the hell are those?' Laura gasped.

Danny had run over with his camera and started to shoot the burned creatures. Somehow they seemed all too real through his lens. His stomach turned as the smell of burnt hair and meat invaded his nostrils. *'Oh my god,'* was all he could gasp.

'Did you know these … *things* … were in there?' Rob said to Tony.

Any hardness to Tony's character was broken. He took his sunglasses off to reveal shocked, scared eyes. 'No, I–'

Tommy sucked in air as an answer to what they were configured in his mind. He said the word with as much wonder as fear, 'Sasquatch.'

'Oh my God,' Adrianne gasped.

'Jesus,' Billy moaned, knowing this assumption was true. The extended limbs, the hybrid face, it had to b–

Then, the smaller creature opened its eyes and bleated out a sound, staring desperately at the humans above it. It held a charred arm towards the burning camper and then pointed a finger in its direction. They all visibly jumped back as it continued to bleat; the sound was like a lamb going to slaughter. They all assumed it was trying to communicate in some base way that the blast had done this to them.

'Blaagghhhh! Blaagghhhh!'

'Make it stop!' Connie cried, grabbing her hair and pulling it hard. Ben grabbed onto her, holding her head to his chest. All fun and games of making a movie had been flattened dead; a gray morbid tightness wrapped each of them like a noose.

'Blaagghhhh! Blaagghhhh!'

The young creature's voice grated like nails on a chalkboard. Tears welled then streamed down its crispy cheeks. It made Rob feel guilt for orchestrating the blast, Danny the same for filming it, all of them the same for standing witness as the creature's innocent eyes begged them from a face full of burnt flesh.

'Make it stop ...' Connie moaned.

'We have to help it,' Ben said, stepping around the smoldering dead mother. He had been in this position before working on the family farm. His father had empathy for an injured animal and would do anything he could to help them. It was a trait passed down to Ben, and fear and trepidation washed around his mind as he came closer to the crying creature.

'It's okay,' he said softly. 'You'll be okay.'

'Blaagghhhh! Blaagghhhh!' was all it repeated over and over.

'Somebody shut it UPPPPPPP!' Connie screamed, her voice reverberating up Onion Mountain.

'We need to –' was all Ben could say before Tony pushed the others away and reached around to the back of his pants. There was a flash of silver, a distinct click, and just like that a .357, Magnum was pushed into the crying creature's cranium. For a moment, the creature's eyes widened as the cold barrel was jutted firmly into its temple. Everything his elder had warned him was true. They were the last of their kind because of the barbaric nature of the humans, and he hadn't listened. He had led his mother to her death, led himself to his own death, and left his father alone.

Tony pulled the trigger. A spray of blood and bone rose in the air and peppered Ben's face. Ben fell backwards, shocked to silence from the mighty blast of the Magnum. He shivered with anger as the sides of Tony's mouth curled to a smile.

'You bastard!' Ben screamed, jumping to his feet, ready to lunge at Tony, then stopped.

There was a collective gasp as Tony held the Magnum on Ben.

'Just try it,' Tony grinned.

'Tony, no ...' Adrianne gasped.

'I have a job to do here. Someone needs to run this dog and pony show, and no one is going near that thing. God knows what it is. God knows where it came from, but it can burn in hell with its mother.'

Ben went to lunge forward. 'You son of a–'

Tony pulled the Magnum's hammer back with a grin.

'This is my set, I'm the boss!' Rob yelled. 'An' I'm not letting you point that thing at my–'

Tony pointed the gun at Rob now. 'Or what, dickhead?'

'Tony come on, man,' Tommy said.

'I should put a bullet in you for the way you keep lingering around my woman – *F.X. boy.*'

'Oh shit,' Danny uttered, throwing a worried glance at Billy.

Arnold began to quiver and sob, everything becoming too much for his prosaic understanding of the world. He began to back away from the group. All the people he had worked with over the last month of filming had broken and fallen apart in seconds. All the good times and bad times ended at this moment, and he understood they weren't friends or acquaintances: They were all complete strangers.

'I'm going … I'm gonna go …' he stammered. 'This is too much – it's too much.'

For a moment, the fear of Tony turning the gun on him held him tight, but he didn't care; he would walk back to California now – hell, he would run. He just wanted to be away from all of them. Then, behind him in the forest, the loudest roar any of them had heard slashed through the dark night.

'

CHAPTER 22

The trees where the roar came from tore open. Branches and leaves flew through the air with the creature's arrival. It stepped out to reveal its massive size, mouth dripping with ravenous rage and eyes flaring with anger. It had seen everything that happened. At first, he didn't know what the figures that exploded from the camper were. Then he became frozen with disbelief as he understood that they were his family. That the pained mew followed by the gunshot was the end of his offspring. The young one never fully understood the evil of the humans. Words were never enough to make him understand what they were capable of: now he knew. Now he was the last of his kind, with no way of ever finding a mate or reproducing again. His kind's entire existence was callously extinguished in a flash. And now, letting rage filter through his great body, it was time to take revenge on those that had done this to him.

Everyone turned to look at the gigantic creature. They could hear its heavy chest rise and fall with every deep breath. Billy babbled, still thinking of the word Tommy had said, 'Sasquatch,' and another name fell from his lips, *'B-Bigfoot.'*

Instantly, they all understood this to be true. This was the thing of legend, the creature that would be cheapened by pulpy paperbacks, T.V. movies, and headlines in trashy magazines. This *was* Bigfoot. And they ... had killed his mate and child.

They all stood in stunned silence, looking at the eight-foot-tall behemoth that began plodding slowly towards them, its feet sinking into the rough dirt of the Craven Construction Site.

Connie started to make sounds like hyperventilating, unable to cry or scream or react in any other way.

Danny instinctively turned the camera towards the beast and started filming, zooming and focusing in on the horror of the creature's face. It became all too real, staring at it through the lens.

Tommy, Rob, Ben, and Larry grabbed the girls and started to back away. Tony swung the gun around to them, his face puckered with rage, and snarled, 'Don't fucking move.'

Bigfoot barreled towards them, coming closer and closer. The only thing between him and the group of filmmakers and actors was … Arnold.

'Oh no!' was all Adrianne could say with a gagging gasp.

Arnold had frozen to a stop, staring up towards the creature as the front of his pants darkened with piss. He could feel the fat on his frame quiver in fear as the great beast grew bigger and bigger as it came nearer. A part of Arnold's movie warped mind told him that this wasn't real; it was some kind of special effect concocted by Tommy as a surprise, just like those other two creatures. That was the only answer to all of this, right? Arnold had officially gone ga-ga. He started to laugh as the beast was almost upon him. He heard his name screamed from behind. *'Arnold!'* All this was Tommy's doing, he *had* done this as some kind of gag! A rubbery grin spread over Arnold's face, and he turned to the others. Sweat beaded on his brow. Reality was a rug that had been pulled from beneath him; fear spread through his body. 'T-Tommy,' he groaned from his open, gasping mouth.

Then it struck. It was no special effect; the beast was reality. Arnold found out at that moment why they called this beast Bigfoot. A huge leathery foot stomped down into his lower back with a distinct sickening snap. Arnold buckled and slammed against the ground, a rush of air and blood spurting from his lips. The creature ground its foot from side to side, popping and cracking coming from Arnold's bones and organs as they were pulverized with the pressure. Arnold screamed now; the sound escaped in a spray of blood. He threw his arms up in the air, clawing for anything that would save him. With one great hand, Bigfoot locked onto Arnold's pudgy wrists and yanked upwards. At first, a huge splitting sound was heard; it sounded like ripped clothes. Then the sound revealed itself: it was torn flesh. Arnold's mid-section burst in a flush of gore. Stringy intestines, reels of yellow fat, and sinewy flab were stretched and shredded as Bigfoot split the man in two and threw his top half over his head in a burst of jiggling organs. The torso didn't go too far; the stringy intestines stopped its distance like a gory bungee cord. Bigfoot reveled in the blood bath that exploded and matted his foul fur. He screamed in savage vengeance; Arnold was the first of his blood lust. Now it was time to finish the others. He roared and moved towards the humans, who were already as white as corpses, leaving huge bloody tracks as he went.

CHAPTER 23

Connie shrieked, over and over again in high-pitched bursts. As Bigfoot came closer, the quicker they stepped backward. It was a direction of escape that soon ended; the heat of the burning camper began to radiate on their backs.

'We gotta make a run for it,' Tommy said.

Tony hissed air through his teeth, never taking the gun off of the others or his eyes from Bigfoot, and then spoke, 'You shit-birds ain't going nowhere 'till I sa–'

Ben lunged forward, grabbed the extended weapon with both hands, ducked, and swung round so that he backed into Tony to gain some control over him. Ben managed to pull the direction of the Magnum away from the group but was unable to prise it from his hands.

Tony shouted into Ben's ear, 'Get the fuck off me, you–'

But before he could finish, Tommy and Rob were on him too. Tommy swung an arm around Tony's neck and pulled tight, hoping to choke him out; Rob came round and tried to help Ben pull the gun from Tony's grip.

'Help them!' Connie cried, digging her nails into Larry's arm.

Bigfoot was almost on them, coming closer and closer. Motivated by the pain that Connie inflicted on him, Larry jumped in to help the others. He went for the only opening there was headfirst towards the Magnum. He went to grab the huddled mess of fingers belonging to Tony, Rob, and Ben, went to yank the gun towards the ground, but a blister of light and a huge explosion stopped him. The gun went off, and a huge spray of blood burst from Larry's chest. A splatter of crimson reached up and smeared Connie's screaming lips. The other women screamed at the situation before them. The melee between the men went limp; all of them released Tony as they took in what had happened. Danny had caught it all on film; Billy was shocked to silence. Larry curled backwards from the blast, his face filled with shock as he hit the ground with a groan. Rob held the Magnum in his hands; he could feel the warmth where the bullet passed through its cold metal barrel. He let it topple from his fingers and land in the blood-splattered earth. Tommy quickly tightened his grip around Tony, gagging the man as he hip-tossed him to the ground. Then the impending reality of the situation loomed nearer and roared: Bigfoot was on them.

Instinctively, everyone grouped and bolted in different directions: Rob ran with Danny and Billy towards the old barn; Adrianne and Tommy took off towards the foreman's office; Connie, Ben, and Laura scooped up Larry and headed for the other camper. Bigfoot wasn't interested in those others just yet; he wanted the man who was trying to stagger to his feet – he was the one that dealt the death shot to his young.

Tony looked up; the dominating presence of Bigfoot stood deadly still looking down on him. The creature's fur blew in the night air; it was glowing orange from the flames of the burning camper. Even in this moment of defeat, Tony snarled at him. Seeing him in this light of flickering flames, there was only one place the beast was supposed to be: burning in Hell.

Tony saw the Magnum on the ground to his left from the corner of his eye. The creature was huge, but was he fast? Bigfoot snorted, taking in the presence of the human that had done the deed to his child as a snarl rippled across his face. His tightened bloody fists uncurled to reveal fingers with spike-like claws.

'Okay, asshole,' Tony hissed. 'Let's go.'

CHAPTER 24

Rob ran ahead of Billy and Danny, remembering earlier in the day the loose boards he had seen Ben and Laura shift to one side to enter the barn. Quickly, he fell to his knees and pulled the repaired boards away from the frame of the door, levering enough room so they could all slip inside. The barn's innards were cold and dank against their sweating skin. Away from direct harm, they each caught their breath.

'I can't believe this is happening,' Billy wheezed, the wire from his shotgun mic tangled all around him like webbing.

'It's fucking happening, all right,' Danny muttered.

'The camera,' Rob coughed. 'How much film do we have left?'

'What?' Billy yelped. 'We got a mother-fucking Bigfoot problem, and you're worried about the film?'

'This is a monumental moment in modern history, and Danny caught it on film! Do you understand what the hell is going on out there? What we got in the can pisses all over that Patterson–Grimlin garbage! We have incontrovertible proof that ...' An odd possessed grin broke over Rob's face, *'That Bigfoot exists!'*

'I used about ten minutes of the film loaded in the Bolex and have another hundred feet roll in my jacket pocket,' Danny said, trying to catch his breath.

'Are you going along with this?' Billy said.

'I'm going along with the situation,' Danny replied.

'The situation! The situation is out of control! What about Arnold?'

Danny gritted his teeth, held his hand to his forehead as if pain had just struck him there. 'What happened to him is awful – but we couldn't help that, it wasn't our fault ... but this ...'

'But what?' Billy cried.

Danny grabbed Billy by the lapel of his jacket, and slammed him against the wall of the barn. 'Listen, you know the situation. Everyone we know has had a chance to grab onto the brass ring; everyone has had a crack at the whip. Look at Tommy, he ain't been in the biz five seconds, and he–'

'Not this shit again!' Billy shouted. 'We need to get Larry to a hospital, an–'

Danny shook Billy hard, pushed his teeth-bared face into his friend's.

'Now you listen to me. I'm not missing this shot; I'm not missing this opportunity. This is a chance for my name to mean something – your name to mean something! And I'm not blowing it for nothing!'

'Danny! Get over here! Look at what the hell is going on out there!'

Danny ran to where Rob was peeking through a split in the barn door, then poked the lens of the Bolex through a knot.

Billy groaned, the full weight of the reality of the situation pressing down on his body like a steamroller. The fantasy world of making a film was over. Now, Rob and Danny had become documentarians. But the lurid grin on Rob's face as Danny filmed the attacking beast outside devalued any such lofty aspirations. All they were making now was a snuff movie.

A line of drool seeped from the side of Rob's mouth as his eyes bulged.

The Bolex started rolling as Rob mouthed, 'Action!'

CHAPTER 25

The Bolex whirred, capturing the image of Tony on his hands and knees as the mythological creature that was now oh so real stood over him. The moment seemed to go on forever, but like a flash, Tony grabbed the Magnum from the ground and had it pointed at the great beast. Just as fast as Tony grabbed the weapon, the beast had one of its mighty hands wrapped around the barrel. There was a thunder-crack as Tony fired; a flood of blood blew out the back of the beast's hand as the high-powered round tore through its flesh. The creature roared at an inhuman decibel but never let go of the weapon. Instead, it reached around the barrel and squeezed Tony's wrist, inserting its dagger-like nails into his soft flesh. Tony hollered as loud as the beast he had just shot, his fingers instinctively letting go of the gun. Bigfoot pulled the weapon from his hand and launched it off and out of sight into the trees surrounding the Craven Construction Site.

Tony put distance between himself and the beast, leaping backwards over the cremated corpses of Bigfoot's son and mate. He ignored the pain that was winding up his arm. He spat on the two bodies that lay before him and smiled. 'Two down, one to go.'

Bigfoot let out a roar and barreled forward towards Tony.

CHAPTER 26

Tommy and Adrianne had made it to the foreman's office and scrambled around the back out of sight.

'I can't believe this is happening! I can't believe it!' Adrianne wheezed.

'You better believe it,' Tommy answered.

Around the back of the small cabin was a small, squared, frosted glass window. Tommy quickly pulled off his leather jacket, balled it around his right fist, and punched the glass out. He knocked any fang-like shards from the frame and then roughly grabbed Adrianne. 'Get in there,' he ordered, grabbing her around the mid-section and hoisting her in the air so she could climb inside. She stumbled in; there was nothing elegant about the escape as she stumbled and hit the floor front first. She managed to roll to one side as Tommy clambered in after and hit the floor where she had landed. The orange from the burning camper lit the office as they scrambled to find the telephone. Within seconds the desk, filing cabinet, and worktops had been swept, but there was no phone.

'There's no phone, Tommy!' Adrianne cried.

Tommy started pulling open desk drawers when something caught his eye and broke the tense look on his face. 'Come on, baby,' he uttered, pulling a walkie-talkie free.

'Yes!' Adrianne yelped.

Tommy turned the walkie-talkie on; a splash of atmospheric fuzz crackled through the air.

He punched the button on its side and called into the mic, 'Mayday, Mayday, can anyone help us?'

Only dead air replied.

Tommy turned the frequency dial on the walkie-talkie, and tried again. 'We need help; we're stuck on the Craven Construction Site. Trapped by something ...'

Again, there was no reply.

Adrianne was still searching through a filing cabinet in the corner when she called to him, 'Tommy, look.'

He quickly turned to her to see what she had found. Inside the open drawer were two dozen other walkie-talkies, all the same make, and model.

'Shit! This is why there is no phone. They all have walkie-talkies up here to communicate with one another.'

'What does that mean?' Adrianne said.

'That we might be waiting for the early shift to arrive Monday morning for someone to pick up. We're cut off.'

The barbaric roar of Bigfoot shuddered through the foreman's office, and they both turned to stare out of the window. Tony and the beast were still squaring up to one another, circling around, poised to make the next move in their fight.

CHAPTER 27

Tony had been a stuntman since the early fifties, and before that, life had been tough; there was no way he was willing to lose the fight with this inhuman thing. Even though it towered over him, was a greater foe than any man he had fought, there wasn't a bone in his body that was going to back down.

As Bigfoot tore forward – all teeth and claws – Tony ducked under its sweeping arms and rolled away. His speed was going to be his advantage over the massive creature. He quickly got to his feet, ran up behind it, and let out four fast heavy punches into its abdomen. He aimed where he thought the oversized beast's kidneys were, digging his fists in sharply, trying to do damage. The feel of its shabby lank hair on his skin disgusted him. The creature let out a howl of pain then swung round to face him.

'You like that, you fuck,' Tony grinned. 'Don't worry, I got some more to give you.'

Bigfoot lurched forward again, and Tony's muscle memory from that old B-movie Kung-Fu flick he had doubled in kicked in. Again, he dodged the beast's sharpened claws, ducked under its reaching arms, and leveled a hard kick in its lower back. The beast let out a howl of pain, and the pointed tip of Tony's cowboy boot met its mark. He followed up quickly with a sharp kick to the back of the knee and then spun on the spot, lowering his whole body to sweep the creature's leg. From the creature's size he would have to use double the force with such a move and did. His shin connected with the creature's ankles, and the impact felt as if he was trying to take down an oak tree. Pushing forward with all his might, he took the beast down perfectly.

'Jesus Christ,' Tommy said.

'Are you getting all this?' Rob grinned over Danny's shoulder.

'I'm getting it!' Danny replied with his own manic grin back.

The creature rose to its feet; Tony was already in a fighting stance. Bigfoot used his height advantage and struck from where he stood. Lashing out with his mighty feet, Bigfoot punted Tony straight in the guts. Its filthy toes rose under his rib cage as he was lifted in the air and thrown back into the side of the one good camper that remained. He slammed into the side panel with a grunt, looking up to see Bigfoot instantly following up and charging him with a curled fist ready to pulverize. He ducked out of the way and took off to the rear of the camper. Bigfoot followed through with the punch and dented the camper's side paneling inwards by two feet with the impact.

Inside, Ben, Laura, and Connie screamed out. Ben had been watching the fight outside as the two women tried to patch the leaking bullet wound on Larry's chest with the limited medical kit that was packed in the camper. Larry's clothes had turned red now, and his gagging, gasping face was becoming whiter and whiter.

'We need to get him to a hospital,' Connie sobbed, unable to do anything with the constantly pooling wound.

Laura tried to apply pressure to the hole to stop the bleeding with one of the camper's pillows. As she pressed down hard, a rasping sound broke from Larry's lips with a spray of blood.

'What are you doing?' Connie screamed.

'I don't know!' Laura screamed back.

Ben drew away from the window and the fight outside and froze as he watched Larry hyperventilate with a mouthful of his own blood. Quick bloody bursts broke from his lips. His eyes were suddenly aware as he stared directly at all of them as if something was coming for him. Then, all at once, his breathing stopped, and a dull, plain glaze came over his face as he slumped within himself.

'Nooooo!' Connie screamed.

Larry was dead.

CHAPTER 27

Bigfoot swung wildly at the air, trying to claw Tony. With each swing, the creature's smell of sweat and dirty fur, and filthy skin entered his senses. Tony was grinning at the creature, goading it with every missed opportunity to seize him in its grasp.

Another long arm lashed out, and this time Tony ducked it, went low, and kicked hard into the creature's right kneecap. There was the distinct pop of muscle and sinew, and Bigfoot fell hard to one knee with a pained groan.

'Are you getting this – this guy is crazy!' Rob yelled as Danny pulled the camera's focus.

'Crazy,' Billy uttered, looking around the barn at the work trucks, noticing that the batteries had been removed from under their hoods. 'Dammit!'

'I can't believe I'm seeing this,' Tommy said.

Adrianne moved closer to Tommy, catching a glimpse of the animalistic look on Tony's face.

Laura was trying to calm Connie as she beat at Larry's fresh corpse in grief.

'Stop! Stop!' Laura screamed. She swung at the other woman, and a cold crack came from her cheek. Connie sobered immediately.

'You're gonna pay for that, bitch,' Connie said, a steely seriousness in her eyes.

'This guy's a lunatic!' Ben cried. Tony was throwing punches at Bigfoot, bobbing and weaving in and out. The massive beast had been brought down to size. Bigfoot became sluggish, visible welts and bruises appearing on what little of his visage wasn't covered in fur. The creature went to let out a moan, and Tony went in hard and fast with a round-house kick to his mighty head. Tony staggered slightly, catching his balance as the massive creature was finally toppled. An audible thud echoed out, as with the killer kick, Bigfoot was finally downed. Tony caught his breath, and staggered closer to the creature that lay unconscious. 'Yeah,' he growled, clearing his throat. 'Just another furry pussy like your kid.' Tony put a finger to his nose and snotted over

Bigfoot's chest with a quick hard blow. Tony took a breath and went to walk away, but as his back was turned, the creature's eyes popped open.

Bigfoot understood the man had the upper hand with speed, so he'd played possum. As Tony walked away, exhausted, behind him, Bigfoot started to rise.

'Oh shit!' Rob exclaimed.

Bigfoot lunged forward with his right hand, claws exposed, and plunged them into the back of Tony's calf muscles. Tony screamed as the creature used all its might to rip downwards; muscle and tissue burst with a pop of hot red. Tony screamed and fell; hot steaming tendons were attached to Bigfoot's claws as they retracted from the gushing wound. Instantly, Tony tried to pull himself away, a trail of red seeping into the dirt below him. Bigfoot rose to his feet. A look of maniacal joy spread across a mouth of sharpened teeth. Tony had made it to his pickup truck now, and unable to do anything else, slithered beneath and pulled himself lengthways.

Bigfoot stomped closer as Tony reached down to feel the damage to his leg. Wet stringy flesh dangled against his touch. He let out a holler of pain, and turned to his right; two colossal feet stood waiting beyond the truck.

'Shit,' was all Tony could whisper.

Then with a huge leap, the pair of feet was gone.

Then the entire chassis of the truck let out a metallic moan as the suspension shifted lower.

'Fuck!' Tony cried.

Then, a rhythmical stomping echoed out. Huge, loud reverberations ran through the bodywork of the truck. The entire chassis was now moving up and down, over and over.

Ben's face dropped as he stared from the camper's window, as did the faces of all the other on-lookers.

Bigfoot was jumping up and down in the truck's flatbed back, either trying to drive Tony out or– There was a metallic pop; the rear left shock absorber had given out, and the suspension had dropped to the floor. Tony tried to crawl out from one side, but the creature's long arms reached for him and slashed his shoulder with its claws. He yelled in pain, rolled back under as the front right suspension point crumpled under the abuse above, and sunk to the floor.

'Oh, fuc–' was all Tony could say. With one gigantic leap, Bigfoot brought his weight down on the vehicle. The entire chassis suspension crumpled like a dead beer can. All four tires bowed out as the truck's chassis bottomed out on the dirt. Every window shattered into a spray of shards. A muffled scream was paired with the crack of splintered bone. Tony was dead. Bigfoot stood on the flattened vehicle, pleasure rushing through his body at the pain he had caused. He held both fists high in the air and let out a primal roar. Then, catching movement from the corner of his vision, his eyes met Ben's as he stared from the camper window.

'Oh no ...' were Ben's quivering words.

CHAPTER 28

Bigfoot leaped from the back of the truck to the ground; there was a distinct thud as he landed. A perverse grin had pulled over his face; a manic glee shone in his eyes: he was enjoying the killing. Human by human, his revenge unfolded for being left as the last of his kind. And in the camper were three more of those who were responsible. Ben pulled the small curtain over the camper's window and began to shake. Bigfoot's lumbering shadow moved past the window.

Ben backed away slowly; Connie and Laura felt fear radiating from him.

'What?' Connie cried. 'What is it?'

'Oh no, it's here, isn't it?' Laura said with a shudder.

Suddenly, Bigfoot started pounding on the camper's hood. All of them screamed in terror.

'Lock that door,' Ben said to Connie, who was the closest to it.

'I'm not–'

The door to the camper was thrown open, and the snarling face of Bigfoot loomed inside. The creature eyeballed them and let out a vicious roar. The bars of spittle connected from the roof of its mouth to the bottom vibrated with the mighty blast. Everyone in the camper let out a blood-curdling scream.

In the barn, the joy of capturing the attack on film fell from Rob's face with a single realization: 'We left all the cans of film in that camper.'

His mouth fell open, whiteness touched his skin, it made him look as if he'd died, and his ghost stood in his place. He could see them now, all the film cans they had shot for *Mountaintop Madman Massacre* piled up inside the little wardrobe in the camper. How could he be so stupid to leave them in there? Time and time again, Tommy, Danny and Billy had said, 'let's drop them back at the lab in L.A.' and each time, he had refused. 'Let's keep shooting!' were his words when this idea was offered. He thought of the business cards he had printed up that read "Professional Filmmaker." At this point in time, they should have read "Amateur Filmmaker."

They watched as Bigfoot squeezed through the camper's door, the jamb bending as his mighty bulk bullied its way inside. All they could see from this vantage point was the creature bent over, unable to stand up to his full height in the doorway, blocking anyone from escape.

Rob went climbing through the smashed-in barn door, yelping, 'My movie! My movie!' But Billy caught hold of him and yanked him back inside. Instantly the two men began brawling, Billy trying to restrain Rob as Rob fought back, punching and grabbing at Billy like a lunatic that had escaped his straitjacket.

'You can't go over there! *You're gonna get killed!*' Billy cried out. He looked up to Danny for help, but his friend had his face pushed to the eyepiece. The Bolex whirred as the images of Bigfoot breaking into the camper were captured for posterity.

Connie bolted away from the door that the creature had stepped in through. Bigfoot tried to move towards them, but his size kept him from coming closer. He became jammed between the driver's seat and the back of the bench seats to the left. Wildly, he tore at the camper's innards, shredded seats, and tearing out chunks of the wood paneling. Connie, Ben, and Laura ran towards the camper's back, leaping over Larry's dead body. They reached the huge rear glass window, and each pounded at it with curled fists. They were like bugs in a jar at that moment; flies trying to escape as a spider crawled in, ready to web and eat them. Bigfoot tore the driver's seat clean from the floor, bent bolts and twisted nuts dangled from the frame as he tossed it with ease to the rear of the camper, just missing them. He started towards them now, punching and slashing and tearing at the camper's fittings to get to his next victims. Ben, thinking fast, grabbed the thrown driver's chair and hoisted it up over his right shoulder with all his might. Tossing it at the rear window, the entire pane blew out in a shower of broken glass.

'Come on, let's get out of here!' Ben yelled.

Ben jumped outside, grabbing the edge of the window frame as he hurled himself out, getting a handful of shards for his troubles. The pain didn't even register in that frantic moment; escape from the terror within the camper kept his heart rate racing and focus drawn from personal pain. Laura went to jump down next, but Connie's hands reached for her hair and yanked her back.

'Move!' Connie cried, as she jumped from the back of the camper into Ben's arms.

'What the hell are you doing?' Ben yelled, throwing Connie to the floor. There was enough room for them both to have bailed out, but Connie had thrown Laura back inside out of spite. Ben jumped up onto the camper's rear fender and reached inside. 'Come on!' he yelled, putting both arms around Laura and falling backward to yank her free. But as he tried to pull her to freedom, a giant fur-covered palm – the missing link between paw and hand – tore down into Laura's back with its sharpened claws. There was a meaty crack; fear fell on her face, quickly twisting to agonized pain. She let out the shrillest sound Ben had ever heard her make. It was almost inhuman in decibel and pitch as if every one of her nerve endings had grown tonsils and all wailed at the same time.

'Noooooo!' was all Ben could say as Laura was wrenched backward roughly into the camper. He slipped off the fender and landed on his ass on the hard ground. Connie was crumpled underneath the smashed-through window as the entire camper began to rock from side to side. Laura screamed in undiluted terror. That old proverb, "If this van's a-rockin' don't come a-knockin'" shot through Danny's mind as he continued to film. Ben quickly pulled himself up, scrambled up to the camper's window, and tried to climb back in to help Laura, to save her, to do … anything he could against the mighty beast. As he looked inside, the creature's hands grasped the top and bottom of her head, digging its claws deeply into her face, turning its grip in either direction, unscrewing her skull like a tightly sealed jar. Her jaw and cheekbones snapped, lips splitting all the way around, turning her cheeks into ragged flaps of flesh. Then one of the creature's clawed hands reached down her torn open throat into her stomach, ripped out what it found, and then slung the contents at Ben. A stinking hot crimson wave mixed with reels of intestines hit him squarely in the face. The fleshy mess drove him back to the ground. He quivered, feeling the life fluid of the woman he had made love to only yesterday splattered on his face and chest. Any screaming inside the camper had stopped, and

the coppery smell of blood filled the night air. Then, with a massive roar, Bigfoot leaped through the open window, his entire body a mass of blood-matted fur. Any loose shards of glass blew out around the creature as it made the leap to freedom with one huge bound. It flew over the top of Connie, who was curled and trembling, trying to push herself underneath the camper's back end, and landed on its feet. It stood upright now, unfolding to its full height away from the confines of the camper. Blood-filled drool poured from its lips; torn flesh and clothing fell from its clawed fingers. It still had that satisfied grin on its face, as if it understood the pain it caused Ben by goring the woman he had feelings for.

'You filthy mother-fucker!' Ben cried. They were words that could have been directed at either the creature or Connie. In a way, either was just as responsible for the death of Laura. Why had Connie yanked her back in? Why couldn't she have helped her?

There was no time for that kind of thinking now. Ben rose to his feet, his breathing coming in fast and ragged. He looked at Connie's wide white eyes peering from beneath the camper. He would never rat her out for hiding there, but if she made a peep to make the creature aware of her presence, by God, Ben didn't think he would stop it from doing to her what it had done to Laura. Connie didn't, though, and Bigfoot bounded towards Ben; he turned and took off towards the woods. The creature followed, chasing with everything it was worth trying to catch the man. As they disappeared out of sight, Connie's whimpers turned to cold, terrified screams as she took off towards the barn.

CHAPTER 29

Running with only moonlight as illumination made the woods a very different place to what they were during the day. Bare tree branches looked like reaching skeletal arms. Owl hoots, crickets' rubbing legs, and the hiss of the cold night air pressed in all around Ben as he fled through the pitch. His beating heart and wheezing breath filled the oppressive soundtrack. That, and the growing lumber of the creature behind as it gained on him. Laura's viscous fluid was trying to dry on his flesh; his growing sweat kept that from happening. Shock from what he had seen happen to Laura pushed him forward; the terror of the creature that was responsible for it doing the same to him made his body move at speeds he didn't know possible. Every stumbling step, every branch that slashed at his face, every vine that yanked and tried to trip him was ignored. Behind and coming closer, Bigfoot obliterated anything in his way to get to the man that tried to escape. Cracks and snaps from branches sounded like broken bones as Bigfoot's heavy footfalls gained ground. Ben began hyperventilating, too fear-filled to do anything other than keep running. The sound of Bigfoot came closer and closer …

Connie ran bandy-legged and buggy armed towards the barn. She looked like a weak-willed schoolgirl trying to outrun her bullies. Tears streamed down her face as her mouth groaned indecipherable words. She made it to the barn door and slapped at the boards with wimpy open hand slaps.

'Lemmie in right now,' she sobbed. *'You can't leave me out here.'*

A hand reached from the pulled backboards of the barn's door where Ben and Laura had broken in; it grabbed onto her leg, and she let out a scream.

'Get in here!' Rob whispered from inside. *'Get down and crawl in here!'*

Connie fell to her knees and clambered into the darkness beyond. Rob, Danny, and Billy yanked her in. 'We've got to get out of here,' she cried. 'Did you see what that thing did?'

'Saw it; we caught the whole damn thing on film!' Danny said, grinning.

'Y–You caught what it did to Tony … and Laura on film?'

Billy closed his eyes and sighed. They had heard the screams coming from the camper and had taken it that Laura had got away when they watched Ben run into the woods.

'Laura's dead?' Billy gulped. His face fell to a dour expression; a black cloud held all around him.

Connie nodded and started to crack, her trembling quickly turning to shaking. 'They screamed at me to shut the camper's door … but I couldn't … I was too scared … and then … then … it got in.' Her voice burst with a low groan that didn't seem like a sound she should make; her eyes glazed as if the actual orbs were replaced with glass doll's eyes.

'You let it in,' Rob sneered. 'What did it do in there? Did it get to my film?'

'What?' Connie gasped. 'It attacked Laura, it–'

'It's a wild animal! If it tore the place up, then it's torn up my movie.' Rob went to lunge towards Connie.

Billy quickly intercepted and caught him. 'What the hell are you doing, man?'

Danny just stood back and watched. He chewed the inside of his mouth and stared blankly at the scene. Billy had seen that look before. Something was being turned over in Danny's head, and Billy had no idea what. His friend could be an irrational hot head at the best of times, but in this situation, he didn't know how hot-headed he could actually be. There was a scuffling sound outside; something was pressing up against the door. They all jumped back into the darkness of the barn, hoping to use the shadows like camouflage and blend in.

Then a voice came from the other side. 'It's us – let us in!' It was Adrianne. Her and Tommy had escaped from the foreman's office when the creature went after Ben.

Billy pressed himself against the barn door and looked through a knot to see the withered, worried faces of Tommy and Adrianne. 'Drop down and climb through the boards on the door. They're loose, and you can get in.'

They both clambered inside, Adrianne instantly falling into Connie's arms.

'It wasn't my fault ... *it wasn't,'* Connie blabbered.

Billy greeted Tommy with a hug. 'Man, it's good to see you,' Billy said.

Rob and Danny just watched them all reuniting, cold, impassive expressions held on their faces as they muttered to one another, 'I want to see where the film cans are. If she's let them get destroyed, so help me ...'

'A month's worth of day and night shooting ...' Danny agreed, a maniac's stare plastered on his face.

Tommy turned to them both. 'Guys, we need to get out of here. We need to try and help Ben.'

'Help Ben!' Danny exclaimed. 'How in the hell do you expect that to happen? Did you see what that thing did to Tony? If not, I got it right here on celluloid.' Danny patted the Bolex.

'You filmed all that?' Tommy said.

'Damn straight, I did,' Danny said. 'We got proof on here that that thing exists. No shitty shaky 8mm film – this is the real deal!'

'Think of what we have here!' Rob said. 'The first slab of incontrovertible proof that Bigfoot really exists.'

'Bigfoot,' Adrianne said as she cradled Connie. 'This is crazy.'

'It might be crazy,' Danny said, 'but it's true, and I got it here, preserved forever.'

Danny's arms wrapped around the Bolex and squeezed tight as if it were a newborn baby.

Tommy sensed there was something wrong with Danny. He and Rob had what could only be described as a Renfield from Dracula look about them: both bug-eyed and twitchy. Instinctively, he backed up slightly.

'What was in that office?' Billy asked.

'Nothing,' Tommy replied. 'No phone, just walkie-talkies.'

Tommy passed Billy one of the small radios. He turned it on and twirled the dial; nothing but dry crackle came from its speaker.

'They're for the construction workers to stay in communication with each other. I don't think they even have the bandwidth to get off this mountain,' Tommy said.

'Shit,' Billy said, pushing his glasses up his nose.

'Tony's truck is dead, and who knows if that other camper will start. It was pounding the hood a good one,' Connie cried.

'We've got the trucks in here, though,' Tommy added. 'They're our only hope of getting out of here.'

'No batteries,' Billy said.

'I know, but there is out there. Tony's truck and the camper, if their batteries are still good–'

'Then we hook 'em up to the trucks in here!' Billy grinned.

Adrianne swallowed hard at their plan and said, 'The only problem is … Bigfoot is still out there.'

CHAPTER 30

They gathered up some tools left in the barn: worn screwdrivers and an old adjustable wrench to salvage the batteries from the two vehicles outside. Slowly they all crawled out through the gap in the barn door, eyes flicking left and right on red alert that the creature had returned.

'D-Do you think it got him?' Connie asked.

'Ben?' Tommy replied. 'That creature is big, but it's slow. Remember where we filmed the scene where he was trying to outrun Arnold? Ben has speed; he might be all right. He might be at the bottom of Onion Mountain now.'

'He might be dead,' Danny replied dully.

'Just be quiet!' Adrianne said, looking left and right with suspicion that the beast had returned.

Connie looked towards the pulped remains of Arnold that lay twisted and snapped at the other side of the Craven Construction Site. The flames from the exploded camper were dying now, but they illuminated his corpse. There was still some life heat emanating from his exposed insides, a natural heat rising from his organs, rising up into the air. For a moment, Connie thought it was his soul escaping to heaven.

They held together in a tight pack, Tommy leading the way. It didn't take long before they reached the camper, and as they did, Rob and Danny broke away from them and bolted inside.

'Don't just take off!' Billy hissed in the loudest whisper he was capable of.

Immediately, Rob and Danny froze to a stop. The inside of the camper had been turned dark red. Bigfoot had opened Laura up, and she had re-painted the camper's insides with her blood. Every snapped off appendage, ripped open patch of flesh, and torn vein had exploded like a burst water main. Neither man had known that the human body could carry so much blood. The movies they had watched – even the most gruesome – had lied. Their understanding of the phrase "Bloodbath" was redefined at that moment. The camper had had a bloodbath, and there wasn't a single spot that wasn't red. Focusing deeper into the vehicle, they could see what was left of the broken body of Laura. It was a mangled shape of raw meat and jutting bone, with spools of intestines yanked out of it. The stink was unfathomable. It was every meat market ever entered amplified, now with added awfulness that the meat was human. As the centerpiece, the twisted off top part of Laura's head sat staring out of the pile. Her eyes were perfectly white in that landscape of sticky crimson, and somehow, still held the quality as if they were staring. Danny's stomach did backflips, its contents tossed like a pancake. Rob's did the same, but then he remembered what he had come in here for: 'My film.'

He waddled forward, possessed by his low-budget cinematic masterpiece.

He pulled back the bloody folding door to the camper's small closet, ignoring the stickiness under his feet and on his hands. It rattled to one side, half hanging off its runners. Inside, his nightmare had come true. The reels of film that held *Mountaintop Madman Massacre* were now exposed and torn to ribbons. Each can that held the undeveloped film were flattened, twisted discs, destroyed by the brutality of Bigfoot. The film was spooled into a heap like dead Laura's torn-out guts. Bigfoot's bloody handprints were all over the inside of the small wardrobe; he must have gone berserk in here and destroyed everything.

Rob twitched slightly, fell to his knees, and plunged his fingers into the ruined film.

All of that work, all of that effort … and all of his father's money.

His father would cut him off; he would have to live like everyone else and work for a living now. Rob began to shake. It was his fault; he should have protected his work. That wasn't what fell from his lips, though. 'That stupid bitch,' he seethed through gritted teeth. 'Why didn't she close the door?'

Rob rose, filled with rage. 'I'm gonna kill her. I'm gonna–'

Danny caught him as he tried to exit the camper.

'Think!' Danny said. '*Mountaintop Madman Massacre* is gone. But we're making a new movie now. We're in this together, Rob. The others don't understand – but we do. You want to make a name for yourself in film? Then this is it.'

Rob grunted, twitched, and then said manically, 'Yeah! *Yeah!*'

Danny smiled, wiping the sweat from his brow. The old desperation that he and Billy had talked about earlier came flooding back.

'I've been waiting for an opportunity to do … something … to get my name out there. Now, this is it. It's time to make a new film. We got one death on film.' Danny patted the Bolex, then turned its lens towards the red mess that used to be Laura and started filming. 'There's gonna be others.'

Rob grinned ear to ear.

CHAPTER 31

They avoided looking beneath Tony's truck; each of them knew what they would find in the pool of crimson that had oozed out from either side. Billy and Danny managed to pull open the truck's crumpled hood with a crowbar from the barn; a groan of metal came as it opened, followed by the collective sigh of the two men. The battery had been turned sideways and split during the Bigfoot attack; acid leaked from its side and pooled on the ground.

'One down,' Tommy sighed.

'I don't have much hope for the camper,' Billy moaned.

'It's freezing out here,' Adrianne said as she climbed into the back of the destroyed pickup and began to search. 'Tony was supposed to bring some of my stuff up here for after the shoot. We were going away to…' her voice trailed off. It hit her then that they were never going anywhere again.

Connie, still covered in the fake special effect blood, stood bug-eyed, looking at the real stuff that had pooled from underneath.

Adrianne worked faster and pulled free a huge black bag, and took out a pair of fur coats. She passed one to Connie, who didn't look up; she was still transfixed at the blood below.

'Connie,' Adrianne said firmly.

Connie snapped out of it for a moment and recognized the other woman. She reached out silently, took the coat, and slipped it on. She hadn't even realized how cold she was; fear had bypassed that basic feeling. Adrianne pulled on her own fur coat and went to swing out of the truck when another splash of reality hit her. She made eye contact with the same crimson pool as Connie had, and the same shock had drilled into her bones.

'Oh my God,' was all Adrianne could say. Tony was dead, and there was nothing that could change it.

The camper had huge intimidating fist marks in the hood, indentations bigger than Tommy and Billy's entire heads. Surprisingly, the camper's hood came open easily, and inside, secured in place, was a perfectly preserved battery.

Danny and Rob walked around the side of the camper, their faces long and distant.

'Laura?' Billy asked, 'Is she …'

'Dead,' Rob said flatly. 'Just like my film.'

Billy closed his eyes and let out a pained sigh.

'We should have taken it to the lab as we shot it,' Danny added.

'That's easy to say now,' Tommy said as he worked to get the battery free. 'But we've got more important things to do than worry about a movie.'

'Yeah, that's okay for you to not worry about the film, Mr. M.G.M. – Mr. Bigshot,' Danny snapped, bowing up to Tommy. 'When you get out of this shit, you're going to a high rolling job, but Rob here–'

Billy jumped between them both. 'Jesus, not now! We need to get the fuck out of here.'

Rob and Danny turned and walked back to the barn, and Billy went after them. He grabbed hold of his friend's arm and turned him to face him. 'What the hell is wrong with you? I thought we went through all this earlier on? We just need to work together to get out of here.'

Danny stared at him, the glow of the dying embers from the exploded camper lapping over his face. 'This is my big chance, Billy. It could be ours if you're with us.'

Rob turned to look at Billy now; he shared the cold expression on Danny's face. Billy remembered when he watched Bob Wilkes present *Invasion of the Body Snatchers* on *Creature Features* late one night as a kid. He had shuddered at that uniformed monosyllabic tone and dead dreary stare of the pop people. This was what he was dealing with now. Something had come over and possessed the two men: Danny's old desperation to live a certain kind of life and Rob's desperation not to lose one. It scared him to think how far they would go. He'd seen Danny stab people in the back in an attempt to get himself higher on the ladder, but he had always been on the level with Billy. Now, Billy wondered who that blade was reserved for and how far he was willing to plunge it.

'D-don't do anything stupid,' Billy rattled out.

Danny's expression never changed. 'I'm looking out for us, Billy. We don't need M.G.M.; we're going to have the world wanting to watch our next film.' Danny held the Bolex tight.

Billy backed away, nodding. He didn't know his friend anymore, and a feeling came to him that he never had.

Tommy had the battery free when Billy came back over.

'We need to get out of here,' Tommy said. 'I have a bad feeling about this.'

'Me too,' Billy nodded. 'Me too.'

CHAPTER 31

They fixed the battery into the nearest Ford truck to the barn door with speed. It had been nearly fifteen minutes since Bigfoot took off after Ben, and since then, not a single thing had been seen or heard of the creature. Time was of the essence, and Tommy worked as quickly as possible. A sweat constantly formed on his skin that he brushed away with the cuff of his leather jacket. Billy stood next to him, checking the walkie-talkie. Still, no other voice came from the atmospheric static. Billy had already checked the truck's tank, and luckily it had enough gas in it to get them off of Onion Mountain.

'The sooner we're out of here, the better,' Billy whispered to Tommy. *'The asshole patrol over there is beginning to worry me.'*

Tommy nodded to Rob and Danny, who skulked in a darkened corner among the thick cobwebs. A low murmur was coming from their direction. They, too, were sharing hushed words.

Connie and Adrianne stood at the back of the truck as the two men worked at the front. Connie was still catatonic but was slowly coming out of it. She was stroking the arms of the fur coat Adrianne gave her to wear. 'It's nice,' were the first words she hadn't babbled in almost an hour.

'It's wolf fur,' Adrianne said.

Connie nodded. 'Isn't it like illegal or something to hunt wolf for fur?'

'Like it's illegal for that monster to hunt us.'

Connie nodded. If only she had pulled locked the door when the creature had attacked. Would the door have kept it out? Probably not. But it would have bought them some time. And Laura ... A thick guilt that burned through Connie like acid made her jump slightly with its touch. Now that was her fault. She had purposefully yanked her back in the camper so that she could get out. She had seen the look on Ben's face when he watched her do it. If Ben were out there, he would always blame her for what she did if he survived, and rightfully so. Another strong feeling set into her mind: she was never going to escape the past. A silent tear rolled down her cheek. It twinkled with the guilt she was never going to escape.

A loud slam echoed out in the barn; Tommy had thrown the truck's hood down.

'Battery's in there,' he said, moving around to the driver's seat.

'I hope you know how to hotwire this thin–' but before Billy could finish, Tommy had ripped off the truck's black casing and had laid a screwdriver across the ignition barrel. A spark burst over the connected terminal, and Tommy smiled – that was good; juice was traveling through the truck's veins. Holding the screwdriver in place, the truck's starter clicked and whirred. With a pump of the gas, the engine caught and purred.

'Where'd you learn that?' Billy asked.

'My brother was a car thief. Remember that animatronic gorilla head I had on my showreel?'

'Yeah,' Billy said.

'All made with stolen car parts.'

Adrianne gave a flick of her eyebrows. She had never expected a little roughness to come with Tommy, a guy who was suburban squeaky-clean.

Tommy jumped from the driver's seat, and said, 'How are we going to do this? We can get four upfront and two in the back.'

Rob glanced at Danny, nodded; they stepped from the shadows. 'I've driven up and down these roads time and time again. I brought that camper up here; I can get us down.' Tommy nodded as Rob climbed behind the wheel. Danny got in next to him, and Tommy wasn't going to argue. Adrianne packed Connie in next to Danny. It was like helping her elderly grandmother into the truck the catatonic way the other woman moved.

'You go up front,' Billy said to Tommy.

Tommy shook his head. 'You go; Adrianne, and I will go in the back.' He moved to the driver's window. 'I'm going to get out and crowbar that chain off the door. As soon as the doors open, I'll jump in the back, and we'll haul ass.'

'You got it, boss,' Danny smiled smugly.

Adrianne climbed up into the back of the truck. She and Tommy took a moment to look at one another. She was covered not just in the bloody make-up F.X. but the sweat and dirt of surviving this situation. Tommy smiled; she still looked lovely.

He grabbed the crowbar from a workbench and climbed out of the hole in the barn door. The night was silent, except for the truck's dull running engine. Tommy stiffened for a moment, the reality he was alone in the barren Craven Construction Site with a maniac Bigfoot running around dawned on him. It was a crazier plot than any of the B-pictures he had worked on. It didn't take more than two attempts to break the chain from the barn door. It fell and coiled like a metal snake at his feet. He pulled the doors apart, giving the truck space to escape. Running back in, he told Rob, 'Let's do it,' and climbed into the back of the flatbed truck. Adrianne was standing, holding onto the metal bar that ran the length of the roof, a pair of spotlights on either end. She smiled, held his hand, said, 'We're going to make it,' with eyes that beamed.

They weren't going to make it.

Before the truck had even pulled forward three feet, something big and meaty flew through the air and smashed through the windscreen in a burst of glass and spurting blood. They all screamed as they understood the mutilated body of Ben lay broken across the hood, half hanging into the cab through the destroyed windscreen. His face was separated into ribbons of clawed flesh; his eyes empty sacs, any ocular fluid had been punctured and poured down his cheeks. Ben might have been fast, but he was not as fast as Bigfoot, nor would he ever be again. The creature had twisted both of his legs off. No meat or bone was attached to the man's bottom half, only stretched and torn skin. Instinctively, Rob hit the window wipers, and in some comically macabre way, the small arms swept pointlessly back and forth, ramming the corpse they could never remove from the windshield. Then, from behind, the entire rear of the barn exploded in a flurry of broken boards. A rage-filled roar tore into the night. Bigfoot was here.

CHAPTER 32

Fractured fragments of the barn exploded all over the truck's rear as a cloud of thick dust kicked up into the air. The huge bloody hands of Bigfoot reached wildly as he destroyed the rear wall, trying to grab anything living responsible for his family's death. Adrianne and Tommy fell in either direction from the back of the truck, both landing roughly on the dirt floor. The nests of spiders that had freaked out Laura and Ben scuttled away from the monster in their domain.

'Holy shit!' Danny screamed as they all watched the creature reaching for the truck.

Rob floored it, a spray of dust spitting in the air as the truck's tires tried to catch terra firma, fishtailing out of the open doors. Ben's body slid from the hood and crunched under the front wheels. The truck's front and back end rose and fell as they plowed over him. Rob winced at the sound: a thousand sticks of celery all snapping at once.

'We can't just leave them!' Billy cried as he watched both Adrianne and Tommy roll off to either side.

'We'll come back for them!' Connie yelled.

'It's time for that thing to eat my dust!' Rob cried, straightening up the truck, getting it under control as he roared forward. The smashed-through window let the cold night air jet through like a wind tunnel. Each of them winced as it reached in and slashed at their faces like a blade. Everything was going as planned; sure Adrianne and Tommy had fallen off, but they could send help. They were resourceful; they could survi–

'Oh no! He's coming for us!' Danny said.

They all looked behind: Bigfoot was bounding for them. Rob punched the truck up a gear and plunged his foot to the floor. The engine revved madly and barreled forward. The entire truck reverberated as it made its way over the rough ground of the Craven Construction Site. Rob found the exit from the site, the back of the entrance sign glowing a luminous white in the truck's headlights. The truck slid sideways as it rocketed down onto the track that brought them here, but Rob straightened it up and floored it down Onion Mountain.

'Go, Rob, go!' Connie shouted as she watched the shadowed hulking form of Bigfoot giving chase. He was a distance behind them but still keeping up. Who would have thought a creature his size was capable of such speeds?

Billy, who was still looking behind, shouted, 'He's heading into the woods!'

'Let the bastard stay in there!' Rob shouted back.

The old track down from Onion Mountain spiraled round. Rob looked at the speedo – he was topping eighty – and steered the vehicle around the bends, feeling the rear end drifting. These speeds were dangerous, but what were the options? He tried to navigate as slicing air through the ventilated windscreen attacked them. Flying night insects that would normally be smushed on the windscreen smashed off their faces. Even though escape was awkward, they were doing it! The Craven Construction Site was becoming a thing of the past as a huge plume of dust rose from the rear tires.

'We're gonna get out of here in one piece!' Connie cried, reassuring herself.

'We are – my film ain't, thanks to you!' Rob shouted back.

'That wasn't my fault!' Connie screeched.

'All you had to do was lock the door, keep that thing out!'

'It wasn't my fault!'

'Just concentrate on your driving!' Billy shouted, holding his glasses on from the force blown through the destroyed windscreen. 'This isn't the time to–'

'Either on this mountain or off it, we are going to having a serious talk, *Connie,'* Danny chimed in. 'If there is anyone to blame – it's you!'

Connie started to wail now, tears rolling down her face as guilt ate her from within. 'It wasn't my fault!'

Inside, something pulsed: *It was.*

'I never wanted to be part of this chicken-shit production to begin with. I should have listened to my agent!'

'Leave her alone, Danny!' Billy shouted from the now whistling wind that hit them squarely in the face.

'Fuck you!' Danny shouted back. Both men began fighting, with Connie stuck between them.

'Shut up!' Rob shouted. 'Shut the fuck u–'

Then he saw it; Bigfoot had taken advantage of the spiraling road down from Onion Mountain and had cut them off through the woods. He was standing in the road, his eyes illuminating like a wild animal as the headlights lapped them. As the truck came closer, as Rob tried to swerve, Bigfoot swung the ginormous tree trunk that he held like a bat in both hands, full force. The impact was immense, a huge dent instantly appearing down the entire left-hand side. A noise like a triumphant roar came from Bigfoot's throat. The truck was forced careering to the right; Rob lost control as the vehicle spun around before crashing into the embankment with a huge metallic thud.

CHAPTER 33

Adrianne and Tommy picked themselves up from the floor of the barn and dusted themselves down. The structure wasn't much of a barn anymore; either end had been destroyed: one by Bigfoot, the other by the escaping truck.

'They left us,' Adrianne moaned, holding her head.

'They had to go. Billy will send back help. We can trust him.'

'What about the others?'

Tommy said nothing, and sighed. Danny and Rob wouldn't do anything to help him. Just what the hell was wrong with those two?

Neither Tommy nor Adrianne had any major injuries from their fall, just minor cuts, and bumps.

'What are we going to do if that thing comes back?' Adrianne asked. 'All we have is the foreman's office to hide in.'

Tommy's head ached as the cold night air made him shiver. Their options were becoming less and less as time went on. He looked around the barn; the other truck sat there, completely useless without a battery. The entire vehicle was just a nine-foot-long paperweight.

If only there was some way to get it started. The battery in the other camper was dead, and Tony had taken the battery from the camper they had exploded. But what had he done with it?'

'Come with me,' Tommy said. They both took off to the back of Tony's truck Bigfoot had stomped to oblivion, and Tommy started rummaging through the wreckage. He never looked down to the pool of Tony's blood that was coagulating around the truck, using the back tire to elevate himself up and into the flatbed. Adrianne paused, shocked to silence as she stepped around her now ex-boyfriend's blood.

'Don't look,' Tommy said, and she fixed her gaze on him.

'What are you looking for?'

'The other battery from the camper we blew up. I know Tony would have taken it out for safety just like he did when he siphoned its gas, but where is it?'

There was nothing of any use in the back of the flatbed. Everything had been destroyed by Bigfoot's rampage, and there were no signs of a battery.

'Where would he have put it?'

Tony was a resourceful man; he wouldn't let something go to waste. Tommy looked up; the other camper had completely burned out and only small plumes of smoke puffed from its insides. The female and child Bigfoot bodies lay dead and stiffened by the gaping hole they had broken through. None of this would have happened if it weren't for the damned explosion.

Tommy's eyes widened.

The explosion ...

He knew where the other battery was! He prayed it was still in one piece.

CHAPTER 34

Billy was the first to open his eyes, blinking away the dull dreariness stretched over his face. He turned towards the passenger door of the truck and pushed it open. The door's hinges screeched as a tinkle of broken glass hit the ground. Billy wavered on the spot, trying to get his bearings. Everything started to clear in his head, where he was, what was happening. The creature was also downed, laid out on the floor in a fetal position. The huge tree trunk it had used as a bat lay beside it, a long line of blue down its length – paint from the truck. Had the creature uprooted the tree for the sole purpose of using it to stop the truck? Who knew? But the muddy roots at one end suggested it had. The strength this thing possessed was intimidating. Billy straightened his glasses, and noticed the tire marks of where the truck had spun out of control. It looked like when the creature had clobbered them with the tree trunk, they had spun out of control and inadvertently hit it too. But whatever damage the creature had sustained could only be superficial, as groggily, its breathing started to become more rapid as it started to stir. Billy went to say something to the others as they started to wake from the collision. The Marantz sound recorder and the shotgun mic were still hanging around his neck, weighing him down and tangling his limbs. There was only a slim chance that they would get the truck started, and they would be sitting ducks when the creature awoke fully. Looking around, trembling with fear, Billy made a decision.

'Fuck it.'

And then he took off into the forest, heading downwards through the foliage towards the bottom of Onion Mountain. Everything was pure black; even the moon above couldn't properly cut through the thicket of trees that were all around him. Blindly, arms stretched out, feet snagging on vines and brambles, Billy, half running, half staggering, disappeared into the night.

Back in the truck, Connie sat up, holding her head. She looked left and right, seeing the two men who sat unconscious next to her. She ran her fingers through her hair, finding a sticky patch she immediately identified as blood. Had she smashed her head on the dashboard when they crashed? She couldn't remember, but the inside of her head felt like one of Tony's explosions had detonated inside her skull. She wrinkled her nose, wiped her eyes, and looked out of the open door next to Danny. She remembered Billy was sitting at that end, but now all she could see was the creature lying outside on the dirt road rocking back and forth as it awoke. Instantly, she was wired back into the moment by fear.

'Oh no! Oh no! Oh nooooo!'

She turned and shook Rob, trying to wake him.

'Get up!' she cried. *'Get up now!'*

Rob jolted awake, his eyes wide and rolling around his skull before they fixed straight ahead. He had a matrix of cuts on his face, left there by the remains of the broken windshield that had blown inwards on impact. Blood had thickened his beard to a matted scab of hair on his face. He let out a ragged cough as Connie pounded on his head, pulling off his cap as she squealed with terror.

'Get the car started before that thing wakes up! This is your fault! This–'

Danny groaned awake now, still clutching the Bolex camera. He wrinkled his face, held his temple, and snorted. He turned to see Bigfoot roll over onto his front and try to get up.

'Shit.'

Rob was cranking the truck's engine now, the starter whining and stalling.

'You and your dumb horror movie! This is your fault!' Connie cried, slapping at Rob like a recalcitrant child. She caught him good across the lips, and his eyes flared with rage. He turned robotically to stare at her, still cranking the engine and pumping the gas to no avail. Connie could see the anger that dwelled inside him, and all her actions against him ceased. Her fear for the creature outside transposed onto Rob. There was something crazed about him now; that carefree attitude he had held during the shoot had burned away to reveal something desperate and hideous beneath. She quickly turned to Danny, projecting all her terror and frustration on him. 'Why don't you help him get it started? You're just as useless as he i–'

She stopped. The same intense gaze was set in Danny's face as it was on Rob's. Connie was trapped, walled in, with each man on either side. A cold, oppressive atmosphere filled the truck's cab that she was unable to escape. Suddenly, the engine caught, and Rob pulled the stick shift into drive with a grind of metal.

Bigfoot had sat up now; the creature was as disorientated as they were from the crash, but it turned towards them with a ravenous grin on its face.

'Come on, let's get out of here!' Connie cried.

'Remember what you did to my movie?' Rob said manically.

Connie trembled.

'I do. All you had to do was lock the door, and I'd still have a movie. But you didn't.'

Danny's heavy hands grabbed her arms and clamped them tight to her body.

'And now,' Danny said with a toothy grin, 'we have to make a new one.'

CHAPTER 35

Adrianne and Tommy moved closer to the blown-up camper, the once perfect paintwork now just a blistered mess of blackness. Tommy had found an old rag and used it to grab the door handle in case it still held heat. He yanked it open quickly, and a dispersing wisp of smoke escaped into the night air.

'Is it still hot?' Adrianne said.

'It's bearable,' Tommy replied.

'I don't think we should go in there. What if something happens? Like it catches fire again? What if one of the explosions never went off and we trigger something?'

Tommy sighed, 'I don't think we have a choice.'

A deep worry set into Adrianne's expression.

Tommy found a flashlight and some old T-shirts in the back of Tony's truck, and now they both tied them around their faces like masks to protect them from fumes. He clicked the flashlight on and ran its beam into the gaping doorway of the burnt-out camper, and they both ventured in. Everything inside was a melted black mess: the seats were all burned down to metal frames; the dashboard and built-in tables nothing but melted slag. Even with the masks on, they started to cough.

They moved to where the creature – mother and son – had ripped through the camper's wall to escape. It was amazing how much power the creature must have possessed at that moment to tear through the sheet metal as it did. The flashlight's beam touched outside, where the two creatures lay dead. Tommy sighed, a single thought passing through his mind: *What have we done?*

'What makes you think that the battery could withstand all this?' Adrianne asked.

'It was all set up remotely, right? Tony would have tried to save as much of his own equipment as possible to use again if he could. I'm sure of it.'

There was still a thin layer of smoke in the camper; they both began to cough under their make-shift masks. Adrianne wiped her watering eyes as Tommy wafted smoke away from his face. They moved to the back of the camper. Once covered in a plush carpet, the floor was now a fused mass that cracked under their feet as if they were walking on black ice. Tommy waved the flashlight around and found a line of exposed, burnt-out wires trailing over the dead carpet.

He followed them along under one of the destroyed Formica tables to what looked like a scorched, metal box wedged underneath.

'Bingo,' Tommy said, rushing towards his find.

It was an old trunk bolted upside down to the floor, covered by a corrugated metal sheet. Tommy managed to get his fingers under one side and prized it from the destroyed floor. Beneath, on a perfect patch of preserved carpet, sat the detonator's radio receiver wired into the camper's battery.

'God damn, I knew it!'

Tommy reached in, and pulled the wiring from its terminals.

'Will it work?' Adrianne said.

'I hope so. The blast might have damaged it, but what else do we have?'

Tommy lifted the battery up, and it slipped in his grip.

'Give me a second,' he said, putting the battery down. Acid had leaked from its side, and Tommy could feel its tingling sensation on his palm. He looked around, trying to find something to cover the battery with to lift it. He pulled back the folding door of the camper's built-in wardrobe, and as he did, a shadowed form lunged out. Adrianne screamed as the body fell on Tommy, who cried and threw it to one side. It was a burnt corpse. A layer of smoke rose from the dead body; its eyes had boiled and popped in its sockets; its lipless teeth bared and black; its skin and blood had burnt together into a charcoal sludge. Tommy fell backward, wiping any remnants the stinking corpse has left on his flesh and clothes.

'What the hell is that?' Adrianne cried.

Tommy held her, staring down at the twisted face of the body.

'A dead man,' he whispered.

CHAPTER 36

'What the hell are you doing?' Connie cried.

Danny yanked her back towards the truck's door and roughly threw her out onto the dirt road.

'No! No! Nooooooo!'

Danny jumped back in the truck, slammed the door shut, and raised the Bolex camera up. Connie picked herself off the floor and ran back to the truck's door, screaming, 'You can't leave me here with that–'

It happened fast. Connie tried to yank the door open, and Danny lurched forward and grabbed the handle to slam it shut. The only problem was two of her fingers were in the jamb. A boney crack and spray of blood came as the door smashed shut; Connie screamed as she never had screamed before, cradling two gushing stumps where two fingers should be. She tried to open the truck's door with her good hand, and managed to pull it halfway open when Danny laid a heavy boot into it. The seam of the door flew back, folding a line down the middle of Connie's face that instantly drew blood. Her eyes crossed with the impact; her two front teeth snapped in two. Connie hit the ground a dazed bloody mess.

Danny gulped, shuddering at what he had done. Rob put his hand on Danny's shoulder.

'We've gotta do this. Fifty-fifty, straight down the middle. We're the only survivors of a Bigfoot attack, and we've got the film to prove it. I'm not spending the rest of my life panhandling in the street; this is my big chance – this is *our* big chance. Remember what Hitchcock said? Actors are cattle. It's time to bring our little lamb in for the slaughter.'

All signs of the easy-going guy he once was were gone now. Desperation had reverted him to something else, something more primal than the creature that was hunting them.

Danny nodded, tried to pull himself together, and began to film.

Connie rose up to her feet, holding her head as a line of red drool fell from her slack lips. Her eyes were glazed and dazed in pain.

'Why won't you help meeeeee ...' she whined.

Behind her, Bigfoot rose to his full size and looked down at her with a snort. His black lips pulled back to reveal his fang-like teeth.

Danny started the Bolex with a small mechanical whirr.

Rob framed the scene by eerily making a widescreen box with his thumb and forefingers. His eyes were bugged out; his grin was like something from one of the horror movies that had inspired him to make his own. Connie realized that the creature had risen behind her, and huge tears fell down her blood-stained cheeks.

'Annnnndddd ... Action!' Rob screamed.

CHAPTER 37

Adrianne started to shake. 'Are you sure it's not some kind of special effect or …'

Tommy stood and held her tightly. 'It's a body. Someone was in here when the camper exploded.'

'But how? Why?'

He looked deeply into Adrianne's eyes. 'The only person who would know that would have been Tony.'

'Are you saying Tony … put someone in here?'

'Let's be serious,' Tommy replied, 'I think we've all come to know Tony was a little unhinged. I don't think we really knew how much.'

Tommy looked out of the gaping hole in the camper's side; the two dead creatures were lying side by side, the finger of the young one pointed to where they were now. Then he remembered the small creature's dying mew, the worried look in his eyes before he died.

'He was trying to tell us,' Tommy said.

'What?'

'The little one – the little creature – he was trying to tell us that someone was in here! That's why they were both in the camper! They could sense or smell that someone was in here, in trouble!' Something sad hit Tommy's face. 'They were trying to help … and we killed them. Oh God.'

Tommy looked down at the charred corpse, then looked around the camper, finding a thin stiff piece of corroded wire from one of the burnt-out seats. He leaned forward, and poked at the blackened jeans that had fused with the body.

'What are you doing?' Adrianne said, looking at Tommy as if he had lost his mind.

Tommy used the wire to pull at a bulge in the front pocket. Slowly, the burnt square of a wallet came loose, and Tommy reached in to grab it.

'Don't do that!' Adrianne said in horror.

Tommy slowly pulled the heat-merged wallet in two, unfolded it, and reached into its small compartments. Awkwardly, he yanked something out, a card, a driver's license.

He squinted at it in the limited light until the printed name on it made sense.

'Oh no ...'

'What?' Adrianne said.

Tommy paused, took a breath. 'It's your ex-husband. Steve Friedman.*'*

CHAPTER 38

Now Billy had run away, they had no audio to go along with the Bolex's images. And as Bigfoot attacked Connie, both Rob and Danny knew that a foley artist could never replicate the sounds of her death. Bigfoot grabbed the bottom of her jaw and yanked it up, forcing her mouth to shut. Her scream became muted, trapped between her locked lips. Then Bigfoot pushed into her, his claws digging into her soft throat. There was a perverse pleasure on his face that grew. Suddenly, her scream became audible through the puncture wounds; the five ventilated wounds acting like new screaming mouths. Then Bigfoot stuck his fingers in further, making a single hole big enough for his hand. Connie's scream turned to a high-pitched banshee wail as her vocal cords were stretched and pulled. A spurt of blood sprayed the side of the truck. Rivulets of Connie's life fluid hit the lens of the Bolex, and Danny instinctively cuffed it away.

Danny realized then, up-close and personal, covered in the actress' blood, what he had gotten himself into. Life behind the lens often desensitized you to what was in front of it. Now, a slash of reality had torn through him at what he was participating in.

Connie's scream became an unbearable high-pitched banshee cry that morphed into a vile gurgling sound. Blood sprayed from her lips; her eyes became dull and lifeless as Bigfoot reached deeper into her throat...

'Oh no,' Danny uttered.

The snap of her spine was quick and sharp, but as Bigfoot burrowed deeper, the sickening sound of wet meat made vomit rise in the cameraman's throat.

'Yes!' Rob cried. 'That's it! All the way!'

It was like he was directing the creature's primal urge for blood. A sheen of sweat covered Rob's face, his grin growing bigger at the massacre only a few feet from them.

Bigfoot ripped Connie's head off. There was nothing clean about the decapitation; red quivering cords held the head to the blood spurting stump that was only a few seconds ago a neck.

'We need to go now,' Danny trembled, 'we need to leave, this is … all wrong …'

'Quiet, you pussy and focus that thing!' Rob sneered. 'This is our one big chance, remember? Don't fuck it up.'

Bigfoot swiped with the ragged claws of his free hand and sliced through the cords connected to Connie's head; they made a twang like snapped guitar strings as they broke. The sick in Danny's stomach burst from his lips with the sound.

Bigfoot brought the head up above him like a prize now; it was free. Connie's body slumped to the floor, spasming now its cords had been cut. Blood poured down over Bigfoot's black fur, and the creature roared at the red warmth of the girl's death. Then he caught sight of the two men in the truck watching him and took a step towards them.

'Oh shit!' Rob exclaimed, as his dreams of cinema verité became a nightmare reality.

'We really need to go, now. Rob … *please* …' Danny didn't want to take the camera's eyepiece away from his face: It would make everything too real to handle.

Bigfoot threw Connie's head to the ground. It made a meaty thud with the impact.

Fear finally touched Rob. 'Okay, let's get out of here!' He fumbled with the truck's transmission, pulled up the brake, and dumped the accelerator. Instead of the spin of the truck's tires, two loud metallic bangs came from the engine as it died. Rob tried to crank the engine to life, but the starter sounded like it was gargling with nails.

'Shit,' was all he could say as Bigfoot loomed closer.

CHAPTER 39

Adrianne slumped to the camper's crispy carpet, a defeated moan escaping her throat. Snot and tears started to bubble from her nose and eyes. 'No, it can't be,' Adrianne croaked.

'I think it is,' Tommy sighed, reaching round to hold her.

She reached out and hugged him back, squeezing him with all the strength she had.

'Tony really was crazy, wasn't he, Tommy?'

'He was,' Tommy replied.

'Steven was bad, but … he didn't deserve that,' she blubbed. 'I didn't want to be with him, but he shouldn't have been … burnt to death.' A realization came as she said the words, the reality that Tony had killed her ex-husband. 'Why did he do it?' Adrianne broke, her moans turning to full-blown howls.

'We can't think of that now,' Tommy said. 'Come on, let's get the battery on the other truck and get the hell out of here.'

Tommy stood and pulled Adrianne to her feet. Her movements were palsied stiff as if finding the body had instantly aged her a hundred years. Grabbing the battery, they staggered back to the barn with their last chance of escape.

CHAPTER 40

Danny regretted everything at that moment. His selfishness had been manipulated by Rob's desperation, and he'd been a willing participant in Connie's death. Now he had a front-row ticket for his own.

'Start the damn truck!' Danny cried as the huge bloody creature came closer.

Rob couldn't risk his new masterpiece being destroyed in the same way *Mountaintop Madman Massacre* had been. Quickly, he reached over Danny's shoulder and yanked the Bolex away from him and wrestled the spare can of film from his jacket pocket, then jumped out the driver's side door, slamming it shut as he began filming the cameraman's death. Danny reached backward, screaming, *'You bastard!'* He was now the subject of the new movie, the unwilling star, as Bigfoot's hands reached in to pull him out. Rob ducked down the other side of the door and peeked the camera lens through the open window as he operated it. Bigfoot grabbed Danny's ankles and, with quick bursts of strength, snapped his legs the wrong way, so his toes met his kneecaps. The splintering of bone was so loud it sounded like a pair of guns going off. Danny's scream shook the inside of the truck's cab. Bigfoot pulled the man out onto the ground, and Rob fell down with him and tucked himself away under the truck's chassis to keep filming. His new vantage point was perfect: out of sight and out of mind for the creature, plus, he had a bird's-eye view of Danny's death. A filthy smile spread over Rob's face, knowing that all he had to do was survive to have one hundred percent of the profits of his new opus. Danny flailed around, trying to use his arms to pull himself away from the creature. The privilege of having upper-body limbs was cut short, though. Bigfoot stomped down on Danny's right shoulder, grabbed his forearm, and twisted the arm to breaking point at the elbow. Danny shot up, screaming. The moment didn't last long as more pain was inflicted on him as Bigfoot did the same to his left arm, cracking the arm around until the elbow let out a loud, meaty snap. Danny looked like an abstraction from a Kafka novel. He had become a man writhing around with the limp limbs of a swatted insect. Bigfoot admired his work, standing still and looking down as the man thrashed back and forth in pain. The moment didn't last long, though.

Bigfoot's huge hands reached down and clasped Danny's head from either side, then with a mighty yank, the creature turned it around a full hundred and eighty degrees. Danny made a coughing, gurgling sound. His body shivered with the final throes of death before stillness set into his bones. Bigfoot made a noise that sounded part roar and part satisfied chuckle. The magazine of film finished, and the Bolex started to make a loud flapping sound as the spool of film came to an end. Instantly, Bigfoot swayed around, and Rob let go of the camera's trigger. Only the sound of Bigfoot's heavy breathing filled the quiet night. Rob became aware that the creature was less than four feet away from him as it started to move.

Fuck.

Bigfoot began to move around the truck in slow, methodical footsteps, sniffing at the air: it could sense him. A guttural growl came from next to him. Bigfoot was standing by the driver's side door. Rob turned slowly to stare at the only part of the creature he could see: its oversized feet. It really was a case of Bigfoot by name, Bigfoot by nature. He took in the blackened toes that sprouted through its thick fur, the long, ragged nails, the blood and mud that had covered it during the slaughter of his movie's cast and crew. The creature was bending down; it sensed he was under the truck. Rob's time was up; his life was about to be over. Then a voice bellowed out in the distance.

'Someone help me!'

It was Billy, lost out in the woods somewhere. Bigfoot swung round towards the voice, let out a low growl, and then headed off in the same direction. A huge sigh passed Rob's lips; he was safe – for now. He shimmied out from under the truck, tried to calm his breathing. He had to get himself and his new film off of this mountain, no matter the cost.

CHAPTER 41

Tommy had fitted the battery they had retrieved from the blown-up camper and slammed the truck's hood shut. On closer inspection in the barn, he noticed that even though the battery was shielded during the blast, the heat had warped its plastic casing. Tommy sighed. Would the battery work and turn the engine over? There was only one way to know. He moved to the cab; Adrianne sat in the passenger seat as pale and unmoving as a corpse.

'Are you okay?' he asked, getting in next to her.

'Yeah,' she said distantly.

'We'll be all right once we get off this mountain. I promise,' Tommy said.

Adrianne turned to look at him. Even that small movement looked as if it took effort.

'Hold me,' she said evenly.

Tommy leaned across the seats and held her tight. He understood the problems she had had with her ex-husband, knew Tony was a safe rebound while her life was up in the air, but now both of them were gone. Bigfoot had turned her already bad run of luck in life into a living nightmare ... *Bigfoot* ... just having that name flash through his mind seemed crazy. He could never have imagined a film shoot would end like this.

'I'm scared, Tommy,' Adrianne wept.

'I know, me too,' he replied.

Tommy sighed. 'After this, when we get out of here ... if you need me, I'll be there for you.'

She pulled away from him, drying her eyes. 'I know you will.'

They held their gaze on one another for too long, and before either knew it, their lips were lightly touching.

'Pray this thing starts,' Tommy whispered.

Adrianne squeezed his hand, and held her eyes on him as he forced the truck's ignition barrel free from its plastic casing. Taking a screwdriver, he pushed it into the ignition and turned. The starter turned over, sounding like it was drowning in molasses, growing slower with each crank.

Tommy stopped, sighing.

'It's not going to start, is it?' Adrianne said.

Tommy turned the engine over again. The starter became slower and slower as Tommy pumped the gas.

'*Please … please*,' he whispered under his breath.

Then, as if luck had hit the truck like a bolt of lightning, the starter caught. The engine roared to life as black smoke kicked out of the exhaust.

'Oh my God!' Adrianne exclaimed, a thin smile wavering on her face.

'Let's get the hell out of here!' Tommy said, hitting the headlights and wheel spinning out of the barn.

CHAPTER 42

Billy ran deeper into the blackened woods, his visibility becoming less and less as the trees overhead thickened into a dense covering. He could feel bushes tugging at his clothes, trying to penetrate his flesh, but he couldn't see his hand in front of his face. He had already planted face down in the dirt three times, could feel cuts and lacerations on any exposed skin, but had no way to avoid any obstacles that came towards him. He had lost his glasses as soon as he took off away from the crashed truck, but there was no way he was ever going to go back and look for them. He had heard the screams of Connie and Danny louder than his thudding heart. That meant only one thing: Bigfoot had got them both. He hadn't meant to scream out, but terror got the better of him. An arched tree root that protruded from the ground caught Billy's foot and sent him sprawling to the ground. His left arm let out a sickening snap, and pain shot straight through it. It was so dark he couldn't even check to see the damage, but suddenly it was inarticulate and numb.

'Fuck me,' he whispered.

What the hell was he going to do? If he continued on, the next thing he broke could be his neck.

Billy caught his breath, tried to calm himself as fear rocketed through his body. He pulled himself towards the bushes that were touching his back and wriggled between them, and tried to hide away. Maybe he could just wait it out, sit here in the darkness until dawn broke. That creature would be out there still, though, and he would have no bearings of where up or down Onion Mountain it would be.

Shit.

What the hell was he going to do? What could he do? Where could he–

Something was moving through the woods not too far away; it sounded like creeping footsteps were coming close–

They stopped.

Billy held his breath, staring forward into the woodland that had become a black abyss.

Then an idea struck him; he still had his Marantz sound kit around his neck. Quickly, he pulled his headphones up from around his neck and placed them on his head. He knew the sound kit's layout by rote with all the hours he had used it; having no light to see its buttons meant nothing to him. Instantly he reached down, found the power button, and pushed it on. A pop of sound came through the headphones. Fumbling quickly, he lifted up the shotgun mic and held it in front of him, scanning the darkness for sound.

A cricket chirped; a slight breeze rattled the branches above; something rustled in unseen leaves.

Billy gulped, turned up the recording volume, and everything rose in decibel between his ears.

He held the mic in the direction of the rustling, his outstretched hand quivering in the dark.

The rustling came again.

Billy listened intently, trying to decipher the sound.

It sounded small but heavy, low to the ground; it was snuffling, moving closer. It let out a chirp.

A chirp?

It was a raccoon.

A smile flickered on Billy's face. He remembered that sound from a short nature documentary they'd filmed a couple of years back.

Danny ...

It dawned on him that he would never see his friend again.

He pulled in a deep rush of air; a silent tear fell down his face.

There was no time for the privilege of melancholia; the sound of huge thudding feet and a raspy deep growl traveled up the headphones wire.

The creature was here.

Billy sat helpless, seeing nothing but hearing it come closer.

Twigs broke under heavy footfalls; deep, ragged breaths filled with snarls. Its rough hands pulled back branches that hung too low for its massive height.

Billy shook now as the sounds became louder and louder. He had no way of knowing how close the creature was as he was too scared to turn the headphones volume down and listen with his own ears to determine its distance.

He could hear the raccoon run as the creature came nearer; heard the creature react as it heard the raccoon.

A chill ran down Billy's spine. Jesus Christ, it was so close!

The footsteps came closer; branches and bushes next to him rustled.

Then, in the pitch darkness, he could finally see something: two burning yellow lights. They quickly cut off and squinted in his direction. They weren't just lights! They were ...

Bigfoot let out an almighty roar, his incandescent glowing eyes rushed at Billy all at once. Billy was unable to do anything. Giant hands reached down and mauled and twisted his body. Billy dropped the mic, but his headphones stayed on. He heard everything Bigfoot did to him. He heard his legs and arms snap as easy as kindling. Heard his flesh ripped from his body in wet, slopping tears. Heard his own scream cut off as Bigfoot ripped off his jaw and half his tongue. As his life drained away from his body in dripping pain, he heard his own agonizing death in perfect, crystal-clear stereo.

CHAPTER 43

Rob lay trembling under the truck, grinding his teeth to shattering point. He had heard Billy's death cries; terror suffused his body and froze it to the spot. If Billy had been killed, it would mean one thing: Bigfoot would be coming back this way.

'Fuck – not now ...' Rob moaned.

After the destruction of the reels of *Mountaintop Madman Massacre* – and with Danny's help – he had made a new film, a better film. It was a film that went beyond the celluloid it was captured on; this was something that would change the world; he would go down in history as the man that *really* captured Bigfoot on film. There would be no denying the creature's existence with this film. He had the Grand Guignol of Bigfoot films. And the only man who understood how it was created – his accomplice –was dead. Preserved for eternity as one of the creature's victims on the same strip of film he used to film Connie's death.

A perverted smile flickered over Rob's face; there was no other person in the whole world who knew what really happened to Connie and Danny. It was only him now, the sole producer, cinematographer, and director of ... *Bigfoot's Bloody Massacre*.

He sniggered again.

That would be his film's name.

With no Danny, he would have the lion's share of the riches and spoils of what was held in the Bolex and its cans of film. That was just the way it should be. He came from a world of money, and now – more so than with *Mountaintop Madman Massacre* – he had proved that he could cut it by himself in the film world. He had thought on his feet, used the upstairs department, and he had three up close and personal, full-color scenes of Bigfoot dealing death. This was raw and gritty work with an edge, not like all that scripted crap he had gotten his dad to invest in. He wouldn't have to slime around his father for money anymore. Rob Lieberman was going to be a world-famous name; he was the man who discovered Bigfoot! Shit, think about those two blackened bodies on his set; if the National Guard or the cops or whoever were called to come up here and sort out the live menace, he would always have the two bodies up by the exploded camper. They were on his set; they were his property. Think what they would be worth to some eggheaded scientist to cut up on a medical slab. Rob started giggling now, thinking of everything he had coming to him … if he managed to survive the night. It was a harsh reality that destroyed the self-indulgent daydream.

'I gotta get out of here!' he grunted under his breath.

The woods around him were quiet – too quiet. Bigfoot was lurking around; the question was: How close?

He closed his eyes and prayed to whatever dark being protected men like he.

'Please get me off of this mountain … please …'

A loud roaring sound came from the distance; a pair of twin lights like glowing iridescent eyes quickly came nearer. Rob's heart felt like it would seize to a stop.

The creature was here, it was …

It wasn't!

The truck Tommy was driving was barreling down Onion Mountain.

Rob's laugh became maniacal. Someone above – or more likely below – was on Rob's side.

He had to be the only survivor, though. This was his story now, his film, and when push came to shove, he would kill for it.

CHAPTER 44

Tommy was trying to keep it cool as he floored the truck down Onion Mountain, but his insides wound into knots of worry. Adrianne was slumped next to him in a catatonic state, her eyes as glazed as the blank moon that hung overhead. She had been silent since they had set off; only the sound of the barreling truck filled the night. He had stayed silent when the dashboard battery light had kept flashing on and the headlights dipped. The battery was dying. He was beginning to squint out of the windscreen, the lights losing their illumination. He had hoped the truck would keep running long enough to get them back to civilization, now he prayed the lights stayed on long enough to reach the lit road at the mountain's bottom. He didn't share his fear that if the truck died, they would be stuck out here in the dark, alone, with Bigfoot still running rampant. The accelerator was suddenly sluggish; all the lights on the dash popped off then on again. Adrianne caught sight of this and gasped.

'It's going to break down, isn't it?'

'No, not if I can help it,' Tommy said.

The headlights flickered on and off.

Tommy sighed.

Please hold out ... Please ...

He steered around a curved corner. The wrecked truck Billy and the others tried to escape in sat there.

Oh no ...

Rob could see the headlights coming closer, could hear the tires rumbling over the dirt road. There was another sound that grabbed his attention, the primal grunts of Bigfoot running back towards him. With no time to spare and mania spreading through his veins, he wriggled further underneath the truck, trying to get to the other side, desperately grabbing handfuls of dirt to pull himself forward.

'Come on! Come on!'

'He got them,' Adrianne whispered, eyes widening at the sight of the wrecked truck.

'They might have got away,' Tommy replied, feeling the lie in his words as he said them.

He put his foot down, wanting to escape the scene, but as they drew closer, Connie's pulpy dead body became visible.

'Oh no,' was all Adrianne could say.

Tommy fixated on it, a cold shiver running up his spine.

Rob managed to pull himself free, heard the snapping of twigs as Bigfoot came closer. Staggering, holding onto the Bolex and the spare can of film, he rushed towards the headlights that now bore down on him.

'Help!' he cried.

Tommy and Adrianne didn't notice him before it was too late.

CHAPTER 45

Tommy slammed on the brakes; the truck slid straight at Rob. Adrianne began to scream, drawn back into reality by the director's face of sheer terror that was coming straight towards them. Tommy yanked the steering wheel to the right of Rob, shooting round him, aiming for the gory body of Connie, then instinctively over steered away from it and lost control. Tommy's truck smashed head-on into the side of the one Danny crashed with a mighty smash. Tommy and Adrianne flew forward with the impact, the pair instantly groaning in pain as their heads were jerked back and forth. Every bone in their bodies throbbed under their flesh. Rob had thrown himself to the ground and covered his head to try and protect himself from the crash. It did the trick; Tommy's truck had skidded all around him and left him unscathed. He quickly drew to his feet, giggling maniacally, still clutching the camera and film. He pulled open the driver's side door. Tommy moaned in pain, hardly even registering he was there.

'Come on, move over!' Rob cried out, pushing Tommy over into Adrianne as he jumped behind the wheel.

Tommy put his arm around Adrianne and held her tight. She let out a moan, and said, 'What happened, Tommy?'

'Rob ran in front of us; we crashed the truck.'

Adrianne started to cry.

'There's no time for that now,' Rob said, reaching round to try and start the truck. 'They're dead, they're all dead – he got them all!'

'Billy, Danny?' Tommy said.

'Dead! Both dead! And if you don't want to look like old Connie over there, we need to go!'

He cranked the truck's engine and got it started, pulling the transmission stick up and down.

'Take it easy!' Tommy yelled, slowly regaining his senses.

'I can't get it in gear! The transmission–'

A loud roar split through the night; the bushes and trees at the side of the track burst open.

Bigfoot leered down on them, covered in Billy's steaming blood.

CHAPTER 46

Adrianne let out a groan as the colossal creature's eyes fix on them. Its stare was cold and piercing, mouth foaming with spittle and blood as it moved towards them.

'Tommmyyyyyy!' she whispered as Bigfoot lumbered around the truck towards where they all sat up-front.

'Rob, move this thing!' Tommy cried.

Rob ground the transmission up and down, a crunching sound coming from the gearbox.

'I can't find a gear!' Rob yelled, his eyes popping from his skull in terror.

With a massive yank, Rob had managed to find a gear that still worked and peeled the truck backward, swaying the vehicle all over the dirt road.

'Straighten it up!' Tommy yelled, leaning over to grab the wheel.

'I got this!' Rob cried.

The truck's rear wheels spun all over the place; gravel sprayed up everywhere. Rob managed to straighten the truck up and made the choice of where they could escape. Bigfoot lashed out with evil savagery, pounding down the front end of the truck with closed fists. Rob plugged his foot to the floor; the truck flew backwards, leaving Bigfoot an ever-shrinking presence through the cracked windscreen.

'Where the hell are you going?' Tommy cried. 'We were nearly off of this damn mountain.'

'There's no time for that now; there's no time for anything apart from trying to survive!' Rob yelled back. 'Reverse is the only gear that works – we need to escape!'

'We're heading straight back up Onion Mountain,' Adrianne whined.

A cold, bleak feeling washed over Tommy: Were they ever going to escape this godforsaken mountain?

Bigfoot's loud, savage roar echoed out as if in response.

CHAPTER 47

The engine whined, wanting another gear to go to as it reversed at its full speed. Rob hung over the seats, looking through the back window, somehow managing to navigate through the dark with only the illumination of the limited red rear lights.

'What are we supposed to do back at the Craven Construction Site?' Adrianne cried out. 'We just came from there! We were almost out of here, and you've ruined it!' She lashed out over Tommy to get to Rob. Tommy grabbed her before she made contact with her nails into his flesh.

'Calm down,' Tommy said. 'Please, just calm down.' There was a defeated tone to his voice, a saddened acceptance that no matter how hard they tried, fate's cruel hand always dealt them a one-way ticket back up Onion Mountain.

Adrianne and Tommy held their gaze on one another. This time there was nothing warm about the moment between them; it was just a shared second of each other's fear.

'What are we going to do?' Adrianne whimpered as tears filled her eyes.

'That's it, Tommy, keep her back,' Rob said. 'Connie already got my first film destroyed, but I've been given a second chance; I've got a new film in the can.'

'What the hell are you talking about?' Tommy asked.

'We have to stop that thing. That's the only way we're going to get off this mountain. He won't let us leave! Can't you see it! This is the third act of the movie – destroying Bigfoot! What a finale! Think about it!' Rob looked ahead, took both his hands off the truck's steering wheel, gesticulated as he spoke as if he was pitching an idea to a producer. 'Bubby, this is solid cinema gold! The biggest box-office draw than ever before!'

'The wheel!' Tommy screamed, reaching out to grab the steering wheel.

Rob grabbed the wheel and screamed back, 'I'm in control of this situation! Don't you fucking try and muscle in!' Rabid flecks of spittle burst from his lips over the windscreen.

'He's losing it,' Adrianne whispered.

'This is my baby,' Rob hollered. 'The best you two motherfuckers are going to get are executive producer credits! A payoff! No residual income from home video sales! N–'

Tommy pitched forward in his seat with a right hook; the blow landed perfectly on Rob's nose. Two bursts of blood squirted out of either nostril as he slumped forwards out cold. Tommy reached over and plunged his foot on the accelerator, took control of the truck as, with Adrianne's help, they pulled Rob into the passenger seat.

The truck was losing power. The headlights were just two dim bulbs that were barely cutting two feet in front of them; the rear reverse lights all but non-existent. The engine was somehow running, though, and through the back window, the moon-lit silhouette of the barn they had escaped from drew into view. Tommy pulled up onto the Craven Construction Site, and headed towards the blown-out barn doors they had only just escaped from.

The truck pulled into the barn, gave a death rattle, and finally died.

'Shit,' Tommy said.

'What are we going to do?' Adrianne said.

'We have to do the only thing we can, exactly what Rob said.'

'What's that?' Adrianne gasped.

'We have to kill Bigfoot.'

CHAPTER 48

Tommy rushed around the truck, knowing time was not a luxury they could afford. He remembered what was in the back of the flatbed earlier and mentally began to plan. He understood how any close-range combat with the oversized creature would end: the deceased cast and crew of *Mountaintop Madman Massacre* proved this to be true. So with what little they had, he began to prepare.

'Have you ever siphoned a gas tank?' Tommy asked Adrianne.

'What do you think?' she replied, her face a portrait of panic.

Tommy grabbed a length of hose curled around a nail on the wall. He threw it at her feet, then rummaged under one of the dusty workbenches and pulled out an old metal pail. He quickly unscrewed the truck's gas cap and fed the hose inside until he heard a splash, then passed the other end to Adrianne.

'Suck on this as hard as you can,' Tommy said. He grabbed the pail and placed it between her feet. 'And as soon as you taste gas, spit in here and put the hose's end inside until the whole tank is drained.'

'Just because I'm an actress doesn't mean I'm good at sucking, Tommy,' Adrianne said in a deadpan, monotone voice.

'No, but it helps,' Tommy smiled wistfully.

Her old sassy attitude – the one he was attracted to – shone from her dour demeanor. The old Adrianne was still under there, buried beneath the trauma of this night.

'We're gonna do this. I'm going to get you out of here.'

Adrianne pushed in, and gave Tommy a quick kiss. 'I know,' she said.

Tommy ran to the front of the truck, yanked up the hood, and began unscrewing the battery from its mount. He took it to the workbench, grabbed a crowbar hanging from a nail in the wall, and began to lever the top off.

Rob began to stir in the front seat, looking left to right with delirious eyes. Tommy's right hook had knocked him senseless; he didn't remember anything while his sight drew to a clear focus. Then it came back to him: the barn, the Craven Construction Site, Bigfoot, his new movie. Protectively, he grabbed onto the Bolex and drew it close to himself like a newborn child. He checked his jacket to make sure the spare reel of film was there. He sighed in relief as he found it.

'You punched me, you fuck,' Rob moaned to Tommy.

Tommy walked over to him, crowbar in hand, and pointed it into Rob's face.

'Listen to me, I'm running the show now, Rob. There is one thing we can do to get out of here: Kill that thing out there, and I'll need your help.'

'Yes!' Rob hissed, his eyes growing with madness like a pair of inflated tires. 'The big finale!'

'Listen,' Tommy growled, 'I don't know what has happened to your movie-warped mind, but I'm not having you ruining another plan to escape. There's something in your head that has gone pop, and you better get it under control because any more fuck ups and it might be your ass getting torn apart next time.'

Adrianne watched their exchange just as the pail began to overflow with gas.

'Tommy!' she called. Tommy ran over, folded the hose, and pulled it from the gas tank.

'That'll be enough. We don't have much time.

'Rob, get out of there,' Tommy said.

Rob slinked from the truck, wide-eyed and wary.

'Are you gonna help us?' Tommy asked.

Rob said nothing.

I said, are you gonna help us?' Tommy cried.

A ray of rationality beamed into Rob's brain. He blinked twice, and the mania that once held there seemed to wash away.

'Y-yeah, Tommy. What do you want me to do?'

'See that old locker over there?' Tommy pointed to the back of the barn.

'Yeah,' Rob said.

'I need you to climb in it, and when the time's right, you have to get out of there quick.'

'Why?' Rob asked.

Tommy reached into the back of the truck and then pulled out a handful of road flares.

'We're going to put one more species on the extinct list,' Tommy said. A twisted smile spread on his face.

CHAPTER 49

'I can't do this,' Adrianne said as she climbed to the top of the barn's loft ladder.

'You can,' Tommy replied, following behind her. 'All you have to do is exactly what I said. When Bigfoot comes in here, make a noise, get his attention, and make him climb up here. Then nail him with this.'

Tommy reached the top of the ladder and thudded down the truck's battery on old wooden flooring with a thud. He had managed to lever the top of the battery off and had used duct tape to hold it in place as he struggled up the ladder, placing it rung by rung until she reached the top. He pulled the top off, and threw the gloves he wore to Adrianne.

'Take those, you'll need them,'

Adrianne put the gloves on, and pulled the battery closer to her, careful not to spill the acid inside.

'As soon as that hairy bastard shows his head over the top of that ladder, throw this in his face. Rob and I will do the rest.'

Adrianne nodded, letting out a long deep sigh.

'You can do this,' Tommy said.

They held a look, each seeing the terror on the other's face.

'*We* can do this,' Adrianne said.

Tommy nodded and climbed back down the ladder.

Rob was dawdling at the bottom as he got down.

'I'm worried, Tommy,' Rob said. 'What if this goes wrong?'

'All you have to do is stay quiet in that locker. Adrianne is going to distract him and throw the acid in his face. I'm going to be under the truck with the gas right at hand. As soon as she nails him, I'll douse him down, and all you have to do is light him up.'

Rob gripped the flares in his hand tight, squeezing them as if reassuring himself he could do this. He closed his eyes, and gritted his teeth.

'Okay,' Rob muttered.

Tommy nodded at him. 'Right, let's–'

'Tommy!' Adrianne called down in a quick, hissing whisper.

Tommy snapped his head in her direction; there was fear in her eyes as she looked at the broken-through barn door. On the floor, cast by moonlight, an elongated shadow lumbered towards them.

'Oh, shit,' Tommy said, then called up to Adrianne, 'Get back!'

She moved over towards the rear of the barn, so she was out of sight.

Rob noticed the shadow drawing nearer now, high-tailed it towards the locker, and leaped in, drawing the old rusted door on himself by the tips of his fingers.

Tommy hit the desk, rolling under the truck.

The shadow drew closer; the sound of heavy footfalls sounded right outside.

This was it, their last chance to stop the creature that had foiled them every step of the way trying to escape Onion Mountain.

The shadow turned to a silhouette as a figure stepped through the door.

Then the unthinkable happened: a voice shouted out.

'I know you are all in here … come out, and you won't end up like old Steve.'

There was wheezing followed by a loud phlegmy cough onto the earth floor.

It was a voice they all recognized, a voice none of them could believe they were hearing.

Blood soaked, broken, and limping, Tony Reynolds stood in the barn's broken doorway.

CHAPTER 50

Adrianne heard Tony's voice, and her entire body stiffened as if rigor mortis had set in. Slowly, she crept towards the ladder and peeked down. Tony was staggering into the barn now, a broken, bloodstained mess. It was impossible; how could he have survived the truck flattening his body? If anyone could have, it had to be him. Tony Reynolds was as hard as nails. He had a meanness running through his veins that held him together like glue. He was one tough bastard, all right, true Hollywood tough guy tough. Adrianne's heart started to pound so hard she feared it would draw his attention to her hiding place in the hayloft. She squeezed the sides of the exposed car battery by her side; if push came to shove, she would use it on him.

Tony looked left and right and then spat out another huge wad of phlegm on the floor.

'I knew you had eyes for my woman all the way through this shoot, Tommy,' Tony said. 'And I bet now you thought I was out the way you could put your hands all over her. Bad move, shit heel. A little dick-drip like you wouldn't know how to handle a woman like her. Come on, Tommy. Get your ass out here, and we can do this man to man.'

Everyone stayed silent.

In the darkness of the locker, Rob began to swap the film in the Bolex. That movie-warped part of his mind knowing he didn't want to miss this melodrama.

Adrianne shifted slightly, poising herself to use the battery acid if he came up the ladder. As she moved, a few pieces of hay flittered down between the old wooden boards and landed to Tony's right. He watched them fall and grinned.

'Hiding up top, are we? Don't worry, old Tony will come up there and take care of you.'

Tony moved towards the ladder and reached for his back pocket.

'I'll make this real simple,' he said, 'You won't suffer like when that oversized fuzz ball got his paws on everyone else.'

Tony produced a switchblade from his back pocket, and pressed the button on its handle, making the silver blade snap free.

He started to climb the ladder. His grin was as gleaming as the blade in his hand.

Suddenly, Tommy rolled from under the truck, jumped up, and charged Tony. He moved quickly, tackling Tony to the ground, the pair immediately rolling around fighting for the blade. Tony held onto it with everything he had, knowing his life depended on it. He could see the savagery that had settled into Tommy, and given the opportunity, Tommy would kill him – all because of that bitch.

Tony managed to gain the upper hand, and rolled on top of Tommy. Tommy grabbed Tony's right hand, trying to fight the blade free. Punches and blows were thrown widely with their free hands as they wrestled.

Adrianne watched as they fought.

'Get him, Tommy! Get him!' she screamed.

She could hear a distinct whirring sound coming from the locker that Rob hid in; he was filming the fight rather than coming to Tommy's rescue.

Tommy grabbed Tony's hair and pulled his head back.

'You ain't got a clue what you're doing, kid,' Tony said, bloody spittle rolling from his lips.

'You're a fucking killer! You're a fucking nut!' Tommy cried.

Tommy's fingers slipped through Tony's greasy, bloody hair as he brought down his forehead onto Tommy's nose with a great cracking headbutt. Tommy gasped, letting go of his grip on Tony's hand that held the switchblade. Tony brought a hard right across Tommy's face, knocking him silly.

Tony repositioned himself to sit upright on Tommy's chest, his knees pinning Tommy's arms down on either side. He brought the blade up high in both hands, arched his back to add to the impact.

'Time to kiss your ass goodbye, boy!'

'No!' Adrianne yelled.

Tommy's woozy eyes suddenly sharpened, darted to his left, to the back of the barn that had been smashed through by …

Tony heard a low growl and snapped around to his right.

There, towering in the smashed-through hole he had created, was the huge form of Bigfoot.

CHAPTER 51

Tony froze, fixed to the spot in fear with the switchblade held high over his head. Before he could do anything else, with a roar, Bigfoot reached in and grabbed the raised hand holding the knife. Where Tommy had struggled to get the knife free from his grip, Bigfoot's brute strength snapped his hand straight off at the wrist. It was a quick movement that snapped and cracked instantly. Flesh and bone split with a burst of blood. Tony screamed, bringing the stump down so that the crimson fluid jetting from it splattered in his face. Bigfoot was on him now, plucking Tony off of Tommy, folding his body up like a concertina that only played the sounds of pain and agony.

Tommy crawled away, slipping back underneath the truck while Bigfoot was distracted. With another mighty roar, Bigfoot tossed Tony's mangled body across the barn; his corpse hit the far wall with a sickening splat.

Adrianne watched all of this happen and let out a gasp. Bigfoot snapped around, locking his death glare on her, and began to climb the ladder to the old hayloft. The ladder bowed and creaked under his massive weight. Adrianne started to rock from side to side as the entire top floor tremored. The battery acid spilled over the lid, hit her gloves, and started to smoke. She could feel it begin to eat into the flesh of her hands but ignored the pain. Above, in the rafters, the spiders that had terrified Laura earlier began sailing down on their silky strands around her. It was like being in a nightmare. Spiders fell in her hair, on her face and body. She could feel them run and wriggle beneath her fur coat and inside her sweater, touching her flesh, using her as a new place to nest. She let out an anguished wail; nothing could get any worse at that moment. Then it did. The foul face of Bigfoot rose over the top of the ladder. It opened its mouth, exposing its yellow sharpened fangs, and roared louder than ever before. It flung out its long right arm and latched onto her leg, and began to pull her forward. It was like being dragged towards the gates of hell. Its fiery eyes, its pungent deathly stink of unwashed fur matted with blood.

Her friends' blood.

All of their faces flashed in her mind at once like images through a zoetrope: Larry, Ben, Arnold, Connie, Billy, Danny, and Laura.

Ignoring the arachnids that scuttled on her skin, face to face with fear, her adrenalin kicked in, and she raised the truck's battery up and threw its contents in the creature's face with all her might.

Its scream was incredible. A deep hollow decibel of pain came from its throat as the battery acid splashed its face. It let go of the ladder and fell straight on its back with a loud thump, immediately thrashing on the floor as the acid did its work. A stinking smoke rose from it now, burnt flesh and smoldering fur. Tommy rolled out from beneath the truck and threw the pail of gasoline over its torso. It looked up at him, lashed out, then held its hand to its face in writhing agony.

'Rob, now!' Tommy yelled.

But Rob didn't hear. Rob was stuck to the Bolex's eyepiece, documenting the death of Bigfoot and forgetting his hand to play in it. His brain had sunk back into the lens of cinema; he was just an observer to the event rather than part of it. Drool dripped down his lips, pooling on his chest and staining his T-shirt. His mind had become celluloid mush, and any hope of being a normal, functioning human had been edited from his existence.

'Rob!' Tommy yelled, jumping over the downed creature and running for the locker. He yanked open the door – Rob was frozen in his vegetate state – and grabbed one of the road flares at his feet. Tommy lit the road flare, turned back to Bigfoot, and tossed it at the creature. The exposition was immense. Bigfoot burst into a ball of fire, leaping up and thrashing at the air around him to put out the flames. He fell into every wall of the barn, igniting its dried boards. Tommy went to try and shout up to Adrianne, but the flaming Bigfoot swung at him. Tommy dove out the way, looked up to the far corner of the barn, where his only hope hung from a hook. A huge bear trap with a length of chain attached hung there. Tommy ran towards it, yanking it down, then ran back around to the back of the truck and quickly wound the chain to the rear tow bar, then slid the bear trap along the ground so that it was directly behind the burning creature. He picked up a long-handled spade, ran behind Bigfoot, and clobbered him with the business end. A long hollow

'Donnngggg!' ran out. Bigfoot stepped backward with the blow, directly into the bear trap. The steel jaws snapped into the creature's meaty ankle and wouldn't let go. Bigfoot's roars turned to howls now. He tried to run, tried to escape, but the chain attached to the truck's tow bar kept him held in place.

'Adrianne!' Tommy yelled up. And with no hesitation, knowing there was no time to do anything but react, she leaped from the hayloft to the truck's flatbed with a loud bang.

She ran, ducked under Bigfoot's swinging fiery arms, and threw herself into Tommy. Flames were crawling all around the barn, and the whine of timber reverberated around the structure. They both yanked Rob from the locker; he started to babble as they dragged him out of the barn. 'This is it! The big climax! *THE BIG CLIMAX!*' The Bolex only let out a series of clicks now, the film inside finished and at the end of its spool, not that Rob had noticed.

'Come on, let's get the hell out of here,' Tommy cried as they dragged Rob between them.

Behind them, the whole barn caved in on itself. Flames swallowed everything in a huge orange fireball.

They continued running, never looking back. Escaping straight out into the woods, into the disorientating darkness.

CHAPTER 52

They wandered through the woods until dawn. They had no idea what direction they were going in, but moving forward was their only option now. The day was muted with a covering of cloud, the sun beneath a dull orange orb. Tommy and Adrianne were still pulling Rob along as they came to a clearing. Either on instinct or fatigue, they all slumped to the ground together. They laid in silence for long minutes, the waking sounds of the woodlands opening around their ears. Birds chirped above, a light breeze swayed the branches. Everything was finally at peace.

'No one is ever going to believe us,' Adrianne muttered.

Tommy turned to her, looking into her vacant eyes.

'What do we tell them? That thing killed … everyone …'

'Its body is in that barn, plus we have the bodies of the other two by the camper. They'll have to believe us,' Tommy replied.

'Plus, we have Rob's film,' Adrianne added.

Rob sat up, slowly and menacingly, repeating over and over under his breath, *'My film! My film! My fillmmm!'*

He got to his feet and quickly walked to the edge of the clearing, staring out into the woods.

Tommy sat up slowly, eyed Rob, and could see he was talking to himself.

'What the hell are we going to do with him?' Adrianne whispered.

'Get him off this mountain. That's all we can do. But that film is the only thing to prove what happened.'

'Tommy, we need that film,' Adrianne said.

Rob stared out into the woods with dead eyes, seeing the images in his head run like a montage sequence. Larry, Laura, Connie, and Danny torn to pieces by the creature. A sick smile flittered on his lips. Gore, in reality, was better than any special effect Tommy could conjure up. Maybe that was the secret? This was how he was going to make films in the future. Find some bimbo on Venice Beach and carve her up with a hacksaw on camera. That would keep the budget low and the gore realistic. He let out a low titter. He remembered a joke one of his father's friends had made about his laugh as a kid. 'The way your kid laughs, he sounds like a fifteen-year-old girl who just found out what a vibrator is.' The memory made him laugh harder. A new vision entered his mind: Imagine the vibrator had razor blades molded in its sides. Tears began to roll down his cheeks now. Rob's brain was broken beyond repair. He had participated in the killings, not that there were any real witnesses to it – everyone was dead. There were only the images from the camera, but with film, he could edit out his blame and inject his innocence. The only problem was he had to live with what he had done. The sounds of Connie's screams bounced around the insides of his skull like an echo chamber. He started to scratch the sides of his head and drew blood, hoping the screams would escape the wounds.

'Rob?' Tommy called. 'Are you okay?'

'Yeah, I'm fine,' Rob replied. It was the most unconvincing thing he had ever said in his life.

Life would be easier if it was a film, you could fast forward to the good parts.

Rob had a feeling that there weren't going to be any good parts anymore.

Then something struck him: If this was a film, wasn't there normally a sole survivor? He gripped his fists so tight his nails cut into his palms. What if Tommy and Adrianne knew what he had done? What if they were waiting for the right moment to do him in and take his can of film?

'No,' he growled, clutching the camera and roll of film tight to his chest.

This was his story, his big finale; no one was going to take that away from him.

'Rob, do you want me to take the camera and those film cans?'

He was right. They wanted *his* film for themselves.

Tommy had killed the monster, had got the girl. But this was his story. Even though the film had run out, he could still tell the story how he wanted to when it was all over. He should be the sole survivor. He should get the girl. He always had a thing for Adrianne – who didn't? She was Hollywood stunning. Danny was right; Tommy was there to steal everyone's thunder.

'It's my film,' Rob called back. 'Not yours.'

Adrianne spoke now. 'Rob, we need to keep that film safe. It's the only proof we have of–'

She should be his woman. A vision of Tommy lying dead on the ground, with himself on top of Adrianne, inside her, slapping her face as she screamed, made more laughter come to his lips. Then Rob focused into the woods just in front of him on the ground. His eyes bulged, his mouth slackened. He couldn't believe what he was seeing. It was as if some great god of cinema and perfect endings had placed a deus ex machina at his feet. All his problems were solved. The ending in his head could be played out in reality now. There, lying in the dirt before him, was Jack Wasson's Winchester 1894 rifle. He had died trying to escape his unborn redheaded child but left the answer to Rob's prayers lying in the woods after Bigfoot had killed him six months earlier. Bigfoot had taken his body for food, his backpack for his child, but left the gun lying on the ground. Rob smiled a toothy grin and reached down for it. He checked the chamber – it was still loaded. Tommy didn't have to be edited from the final cut; he could be blown from the negative.

'Oh, Tommy!' Rob called, turning to face them with the rifle butted in his shoulder. 'I've got something you can have.'

CHAPTER 53

Tommy and Adrianne froze to the spot, their mouths agape. They hadn't seen where the rifle had come from; from their point of view, it had just appeared in Rob's hands like a jump cut in a film. Rob pushed his face to the metal barrel, putting Tommy squarely in the gun's sights.

'This is my film, Tommy,' he growled. 'And you didn't make the final cut.'

Adrianne yelled, 'Rob, no!' But it was too late.

Rob pulled the Winchester's trigger, and a huge explosion echoed out around the woods.

Tommy closed his eyes, gritted his teeth, raised his hands instinctively to shield himself from the rifle's round, and stood there waiting for impact.

It never came.

Adrianne screamed.

Slowly, Tommy opened his eyes. Rob dropped the rifle, swayed from left to right on the spot. All the fingers on Rob's right hand were blown to pulpy stumps; the side of his face he had pushed to the barrel was now a mask of bloody ripped flesh. Tommy could see his jaw and teeth exposed through the ragged hole in his face. Rob's right eye that he'd used to aim the gun was now just a pouring socket of gore. Rob fell to his knees, held out his fingerless hand towards them as if asking for help, then fell face-first on the ground, dead.

'What the hell happened?' Adrianne sobbed.

Tommy moved closer to Rob's body, his heart machine-gunning in his chest. He could smell a damp sulphury smell in the air.

'The gun backfired,' Tommy sighed.

After six months of lying on the floor of Onion Mountain, the Winchester's ammunition had got wet, and the round loaded into the rifle's barrel had blown up in Rob's face.

Tommy reached around Rob's dead body, unstrapped the Bolex from his shoulder, and took the film can from inside his jacket. A gurgling sound came up Rob's throat. It was like his last attempt to warn Tommy the film was his.

'We need to keep moving,' Tommy said, getting to his feet and embracing Adrianne.

They walked away, leaving Rob's corpse as flies began to hover over it.

The sun started to break through the clouds, and the shade from the branches above did little to aid them. They had no water, and their throats became rough. Exhaustion and fatigue were as palpable as the growing humidity around them. Neither Tommy nor Adrianne had any idea where they were headed; the landscape was an endless mass of tightly packed trees and ferns. They said nothing to one another for what felt like hours. Then Adrianne gasped.

'What is it?' Tommy snapped.

'There,' Adrianne replied.

She pointed forward through the trees to a vanishing point where the sun's rays poured down: It was the end of the woodland that surrounded them. They both began to run, jumping over felled branches and vines that tried to trip them, moving closer to their escape. Making it to the end of the woods, Adrianne screamed, 'Tommy!'

Tommy skidded to a halt, staring down as he exited the woodland. He caught his balance and fell back on his ass. It wasn't just the end of the woods; it was the start of a sheer drop straight down one side of Onion Mountain. Adrianne fell next to him, grabbing him. 'Oh my God, are you okay?' she asked.

Tommy nodded, looking over the edge of the cliff to a collection of jagged grey rocks fifty feet below. They had unknowingly been traveling up Onion Mountain all night, and before them, beyond the dangerous rocks below, was a sprawling landscape of more dense trees.

'We're never going to escape,' Adrianne moaned. 'What are we going to do?'

Tommy swallowed, his throat feeling as if he'd been swallowing sand. He looked into the distance, shielding his eyes from the sun above and gasped. Smokestacks were spewing fumes into the sky on the horizon.

It can't be ...

It was some kind of factory or mill or … who the hell cared? It was civilization!

'There!' he said, pointing in the direction of his discovery.

Adrianne looked to where he gestured and understood. She began to laugh, and it became infectious, both of them letting rip with laughter.

'We made it,' Tommy gasped. He put the Bolex and the film can on the floor next to him and laid on his back. 'We escaped.'

'I can't believe it,' Adrianne grinned.

'No matter what happens now, we have the film; we have proof of what happened last night. It'll corroborate our story. No one can ever call us cranks or disbelieve us.' Tommy sat up, looking at Adrianne. 'You know what the authorities are like; you know they would try and pin Laura, Billy, or Larry on us. But they can't if we have this.' Tommy grabbed the Bolex, shook it, and placed it back on the ground.

Adrianne looked at the camera, her eyes never moving from Tommy.

'Hold me,' she said, standing up and holding out her arms to Tommy.

He stood and held her, squeezing her tight.

'I'll look after you now,' Tommy said. 'It'll be all right; I'll look after you.'

They came apart. Adrianne stared deeply into Tommy's eyes.

'It's okay,' she said. 'I'll look after myself.'

'What do you me–'

Before Tommy had finished his response, Adrianne thrust forward and pushed him off the cliff's edge.

CHAPTER 54

Tommy hung from the cliff's edge, his fingers digging into hard rock, trying to keep a grip as his feet dangled. He looked up; Adrianne was stood looking down at him. Her face was dull and sullen; she showed no emotion towards the man she had bonded with for the past twenty-four hours.

'I told you that you end up doing things you'd never expect, Tommy. I need money; I need to live a certain kind of lifestyle, and this acting crap just isn't cutting the mustard. I knew Steve was tied up in that camper when it blew; that was the plan. I needed a certain kind of man to do a certain kind of job, and I found him. Tony was nuts, but I could use him. All I had to do was set Steve up to look like he was the nutty one, stalking me on set, hiding out in the camper, and then KA-BLAM! Insurance payout city! That was until those fucking creatures turned up.'

'You don't have to do this,' Tommy wheezed, trying to pull himself up to safety.

'Yeah, I really *really* do,' Adrianne sighed. 'When Tony fell through, well … I used you, Tommy. You're cute and all, but … I don't want you. Like I said, I don't want to be shacked up and tied down with a kid. I have my whole life in front of me! And I can tell you are one of those guys that thinks he can go walking into the sunset with a beautiful woman on his arm and all that normal crap in his future. Well, not with me! I want freedom! I want financial security! And if *I'm* the sole survivor of a Bigfoot attack, and *I* have the film to prove it, well, I'm going to get everything I want. No fifty-fifty split. No second billing. I'm going to be the owner of the most important story and piece of footage that has ever existed.'

Adrianne smiled. 'If I would have known that two months ago, old Steve wouldn't have had to be the main course at the cookout.'

'Adrianne, pull me up. You can keep the film. I know you don't want to do this to me.'

'Oh, Tommy, you just don't get it, do you? Guys like you never do.'

Tears welled in Tommy's eyes, and Adrianne pulled an awkward smile, knowing she should feel something, even though she felt nothing.

'I know you like me, Tommy, so just close your eyes and remember the good times.'

'Oh, n–'

Before Tommy could say any more, Adrianne raised her foot up and brought it down into Tommy's face. There was a crack as his nose broke, his hands instinctively loosening from the rock, wanting to protect his face.

Tommy fell, letting out a cold petrified scream that quickly ended with a bone-chilling snap. His voice trailed off in echo around Onion Mountain; it sounded like his spirit had left his body and was trying to make its way to Heaven. Adrianne looked over the cliff's edge; Tommy had been impaled on one of the sharpened rocks below, a huge grey spike protruded through the front of his chest. Blood and gore had splattered out of the wound and was dripping down on the rocks around him.

'Bye, Tommy,' Adrianne said, reaching down to pick up the Bolex and the can of film. All she had to do now was stay focused and walk towards where smoke billowed on the horizon. No one would ever know when Tommy died; she could blame that on Bigfoot too.

'Bigfoot ...' she whispered condescendingly.

The silence around her was broken. The ferns and tree branches behind her burst open, and a huge roaring form lumbered out. Adrianne stepped backward, stopping before she joined Tommy at the bottom of the cliff.

It can't be; we killed it!

The burnt, bloody figure of Bigfoot leered down at her. Its hair was almost gone; only black nubbed patches and pulsating boils remained over its enormous body. One eye was now a fried white orb from the battery acid she had thrown in its face. The ankle Tommy had caught with the bear trap was a glistening red mess. Somehow he had managed to escape the barn fire. Then she remembered the water trough at the back of the barn; the creature had somehow climbed inside to douse out the flames that ravaged it. That was the only explanation. Bigfoot had its mate and child slumped over its mighty shoulders and threw their limp, dead bodies at its feet. He was ascending Onion

Mountain with them, was going to give them a burial outside his cave. Bigfoot let out another roar and reached out for Adrianne. She screamed, dropped the Bolex and film cans over the cliff's edge. Both the camera and film cans exploded, the celluloid exposed and useless now, the sunlight bleaching its frames to blankness. Bigfoot grabbed Adrianne by her arms and lifted her in the air, her feet kicking beneath her as she went, as he slowly brought her face to face with him. She was inches away from it. The creature's fetid breath washed through her senses as she was forced to stare into its disgusting scabrous visage. Its slitted nose sniffed at Adrianne as its rough hands kneaded the arms of her fur coat. It understood she was the only survivor. In a way, she was like it: The last survivor of her own kind. It could smell her woman heat radiating from beneath her soiled clothes, and an idea formed in its pain-addled brain.

It kneaded her fur coat more softly now.

She had taken away its family, had made sure that its bloodline ended.

She would have to pay for the humans' mistakes.

It would never be as pure a bloodline as it had been with his original mate, but maybe his kind could live on.

A tendril of drool poured from the creature's blackened lips; another part of it burnt in the fire began to swell back to life.

'Please ...' was all Adrianne could say, sensing what the huge creature had in store for her.

She murmured as Bigfoot tightened his grip on her arms, bringing her face down closer to his own. Its slug-like tongue moved towards her as it grinned.

'Oh no!'

CHAPTER 56

NINE MONTHS LATER

Onion Mountain sat silently, all of the drama from almost a year ago fading into the past. The police had found the burned-out barn, the wrecked campers and trucks, and the bodies of all the kids that had been making a movie. It was a slow gruesome process putting the bodies back together scattered through the woods and around the Craven Construction Site. Rob's original film, now lost to the flames of the wrecked camper, had received some free publicity he could have never imaged on the front cover of *Weekly World News. "Mountaintop Madman Massacre – BLOOD BATH!"* was splashed over the paper a week after the incident. Other newspapers focused on the missing Adrianne Heather Curtis and how the cast of the unfinished film fell foul to a drug baron's goons associated with her husband, Steve Friedman. No self-respecting paper printed the more speculative elements that surrounded the case. For every irregularity that stood out, the mainstream media – with the help of Adrianne's father's checkbook – brushed aside the absurdities the *Weekly World News* reveled in.

The strange, oversized footprints found around the Craven Construction Site were written off as special effect gimmicks from the horror movie they were making.

The strength needed to perform the mutilations on the bodies wasn't just the work of one savage man – that was impossible – it was a group of savage men.

The tuft of wiry hair that was found caught on the flattened truck where a pool of Tony Reynolds' blood was beneath was fobbed off as a bear's.

That was the second theory proposed, that the whole production had fallen foul of a bear. A great big eighteen-foot grizzly had wandered onto the set and made the cast and crew its own personal craft services table.

That wasn't what the *Weekly World News* went in for, though. They smelled a cover-up when no one else did; they understood a truth that no one else was reporting on. There was another answer to what had happened, a more obvious answer if you thought outside the box and were open to the possibilities of alien abduction, reptile people running the government, and vampires living in the New York City subway tunnels. If you believed all of those things, then their answer to what happened with the production of *Mountaintop Madman Massacre* was simple.

Bigfoot.

Yeah ... right.

Thomas Curtis, Adrianne's father, had hit them with a lawsuit so hard it had made the chief editor's head spin. They had redacted the article, had made a public apology for printing such tripe. Thomas was a proud man who knew his daughter's problems, mixed up with drink and drugs and scum like Steve Friedman, but he was never going to let his daughter's name be mixed up with all that Bigfoot nonsense; that was a step too far.

Now, nine months later, Thomas hiked alone up Onion Mountain. He had hired trackers, guides, but none of them had found any trace of his daughter. There was a part of him that sensed she was still on Onion Mountain. He didn't know why, call it instinct or intuition, but there was a gut feeling ... she was out there somewhere.

He climbed nearer the peak of Onion Mountain towards rocky terrain, higher than any of the paid professionals were willing to go. Suddenly he was giddy. He was sixty-five years old, and a realization hit him: He shouldn't be up here, doing this. There was no way Adrianne was on top of Onion Mountain. A jolt of despair hit his heart like an arrow; it poisoned him with the acceptance she was gone forever.

Thomas let out a sigh, and began to climb back down the cold grey rocks.

A sound cut through the hollow wind around him. It was a mewing wail, which could almost be ... human.

He stopped, listened.

Silence.

It must have been some animal ...

Then he made his way slowly down the side of the mountain. If he had climbed only a little higher, had found the opening to the hidden cave on the next ridge up, all of his answers would have been answered. He would have found Adrianne, would have understood his instinct was right; she was still on Onion Mountain. He would have known everything, even that the mewing he heard wasn't just an animal, that it *was* part human. He would have also found out the *Weekly World News* was right.

There could have been a family reunion on Onion Mountain.

Thomas, Adrianne … and her new son …

A creature, half-human, half-Bigfoot, let out another piercing cry.

THE END

ALSO FROM SEVERED PRESS:
DAVID IRONS'
POLYBIUS

CHAPTER 1
PORTLAND, OREGON – FRIDAY, OCTOBER 30TH, 1981 – 6.11 A.M.

The morning was quiet, no different from any other morning.

In a way, this morning was like the contents of the matte grey Ford shipping truck that rumbled through the suburbs of Portland, Oregon with its single delivery. Looks could be deceiving.

Kids stirred in their beds, dreaming of wearing their Halloween costumes the coming weekend. Moms and dads awoke, prepared for another day of doing the same old thing at work.

Inconspicuously, the most inconspicuous thing on the road that morning stayed to all the speed limits, used its turn signals for every corner, and stopped a good ten feet behind every red light.

Everything was immaculate on the truck, showroom new, mechanically perfect: the starter motor never over-cranked, the alternator hardly ever generated any power; the exhaust's innards un-blackened, still silver with newness; new tires – not even a millimetre's worth of wear on them.

Slowly, the truck made its way through the sleepy streets towards its destination, its headlights looming like demonic eyes. It crossed the Burlington Northern Railroad Bridge, the Willamette River beneath looking like a darkened screen rippling with waves of static.

Inside the truck's cab, two men sat in silence, the man on the passenger's side black and in his mid-twenties, the driver white, ten years older, his hair a lightly greying blond. Their jumpsuits were a dull charcoal grey colour coordinated with the truck, each uniform sporting a matching embroidered white logo on the left lapel, the same as the printed white logo on the truck's vinyl-curtained sides: SINNESLÖSCHEN.

The truck rumbled off the bridge, reaching Doane Point. Lights burned from the warehouses to the right; smoke rose from the Metro Central hazardous waste plant to the left. The vehicle stealthily crept towards St Helens Road, then slid to a stop in a deserted parking lot.

Rural, isolated, segregated from the rest of Portland.

The high schools and the university only a stone's throw away.

For tonight, the location was perfect.

A veil of fog had fallen during the night, a natural shroud to the secrecy.

The truck's doors opened. The two men stepped out, a few new creases in their previously unused jumpsuits. They worked in precision, each movement rehearsed and choreographed, opening the truck's back doors as carefully as a superstitious man would open a tomb.

They climbed in.

The blond man punched a button. The truck's tail lift moved into position. Then the men hesitated, each hoping in some way the other would dare to be the first to touch the cargo.

The black man finally spoke: 'Come on, let's just do it.'

Reluctantly, they simultaneously grabbed the jet-black arcade cabinet, their hands protected with thick work gloves.

There were no distinguishable markings on the machine's sides; no stickers or name on the marquee. It was a phantom cabinet, a black ghost with no name.

Generic black joystick.

Generic single-fire button.

Loading the cabinet onto a lifting trolley, the men lowered the machine to the asphalt with the truck's tail lift as gently as they would a neutron bomb.

Then they began to drag the trolley across the parking lot, both looking over their shoulders suspiciously as they went, two perturbed figures wandering in the morning mists.

A hot-pink neon sign sizzled into view – JERRY'S ARCADE – blazing on a two-story building, once an old laundry mill, now updated for the '80s.

The men navigated towards the huge glass panels that stretched around three of the building's four sides, lines of arcade machines visible inside, all sitting in silence, like rows of electronic coffins.

A black Ford Econoline box van pulled up in front of the arcade, appearing through the mists as if conjured from beneath a magician's cape. Two men jumped out and approached the arcade, both in black – dark glasses and dark suits. The taller man, bearded, his hair shoulder length, evenly parted in the middle – handsome in a way – produced a ring of keys, opened the arcade's glass-panelled doors, and quickly moved inside.

He hissed to the deliverymen in a German accent: *'Schneller.'*

The German's companion in black stood by the door, holding it open for the deliverymen and the machine. Now he did the suspicious looking around.

The deliverymen followed the German as he walked in front of them, consulting a clipboard with a blueprint of the arcade attached to it, guiding the jet-black cabinet past rows of video games: *Pac-Man, Space Invaders, Rally X, Defender, Phoenix.*

He pointed to an opening in the lined-up machines.

'Here.'

Swiftly, the two deliverymen pushed the new machine in place, perfectly slotting it into its new home.

It sat neutrally next to the other video games, a shadow compared to the garish facades of other machines around it.

The black deliveryman shimmied around to the cabinet's back and plugged its power cord into the mains.

The German took a handheld device from his pocket, pulled a telescopic chromed aerial free from it, and pressed a button.

A low hum immediately radiated to life inside the black cabinet, growing in decibels, then settling to a whispering growl.

He smiled slyly, inhaling a breath with only a hint of worry buried inside it.

Diagnostic numbers burst to life on the screen before him, leaving electron dots of light burning as they disappeared.

'So fängt es an ...'

And so it begins ...

Suddenly, the new machine's black marquee popped to life with light. Yellow and green text illuminated from behind spelled out the machine's name:

POLYBIUS

A momentary ear-piercing chime sounded, as high-pitched as a dog whistle, yet somehow still audible to human ears.

The men all gritted their teeth, squinted their eyes.

The German pushed the button on the handheld device again: the machine quieted; the screen turned black.

'Come on, let's get out of here,' the German said.

He started to walk away, stopped, turned to the deliverymen with a friendly expression. 'Coffee?' he asked.

The workers nodded. 'Sounds great, Mr. Röach,' the truck's driver said.

They quickly made their way outside.

As they exited the arcade, Steven Röach threw one final look back at the newly installed machine, the sly smile back on his face.

It was ready, it was waiting, and everything had gone to plan.

Now all the machine needed was players.

It was Friday morning.

Friday night was coming.

The high schools and university were so close, only over the bridge.

The players would be here … soon.

That's when the fun would begin.

AND:
DAVID IRONS'
NIGHT CREEPERS

Summertime – 1998

'Six bucks, what the hell can you even buy with six bucks?' Peter Carey threw the broom across the dusty old shed, watched as it rebounded off the mountainous stack of newspapers piled to the old sagging roof.

Sarah Jones, the girl who always had blonde pigtails and chewed gum, laughed, clapping her hands and watching the vaporous mist of dust motes explode from her fingers in the afternoon sun.

The pair of them had been recruited by their moms to clear out old Mrs. Baker's shed; well, shed seemed too posh a word for the derelict shack they stood in now. It was the size of an apartment, three well spaced rooms brimming with archaic debris from the old woman's life: crystal radio sets, valve TV sets, grandfather clocks with sprung innards. The years old stench of rot attacked the insides of their nostrils as if festering cacti had been inserted into them; the taste at the back of their throats a dry woody tang.

'Six bucks, what's it worth?' Peter said. 'A McDonalds and a comic book? A few games down at the arcade? A ticket to see some bullshit movie? Fuck me, if I asked my old man for that chump-change he would toss it to me.' He spat, watching it instantly dissolve into the dust sodden floor, vanishing in its dryness as if it had never been there.

Another voice entered the conversation, one that turned both their faces sour. 'It's not bad, I mean our moms did ask us to help Mrs. Baker. I didn't even know we were getting paid,' Jennifer Blu said.

'Shut up,' Peter sneered, as Sarah shook her head, face puckered as her pigtails hit her cheeks. The three of them were acquainted with one another from school, Peter and Sarah being friends from fifth grade, Jennifer Blu a new arrival six months ago in seventh grade. She had even moved into Max Foster's house at the end of the block. Max was one of the guys — one of the boys. Max was the kid all the girls called a babe, or hot stuff.

Now, Max was gone — moved to Idaho, and his replacement... the scrawny red-haired girl that stood before them now.

Jennifer knew the eyes they gave her, they were one of the most pervasive things in her time here in California. The same eyes transferring from skull to skull, face to face, eyes that said 'Who are *you,* Jennifer *Blu?'* Not one of them — that was for sure. God, she missed Boston. Why couldn't they have stayed in Boston?

'You'll fit in, honey, it just takes time!' Mom said.

'It's normal to be the odd one out to begin with, until someone new comes along and they become the odd one out,' Dad had said.

Time had passed, other new kids had come, but her ridicule hadn't gone.

'Maybe, we can turn you upside down and use that ginger mop to sweep the floor with, Jennifer,' Peter grinned.

'Yeah, like go put a fucking hat on, your hair is hurting my eyes,' Sarah groaned. 'It's offensive.'

'Good one!' Peter snorted.

Jennifer clenched her fists three times, words echoing in her mind — *Ignore it. Ignore It. Ignore it.*

'I'm done with this B.S.,' Peter said, hawking another loogie on the floor. 'Tell the old bag she can keep the six bucks, I've had it.'

'Yeah, really,' Sarah said, rolling her eyes.

'Hey, come on, we can't let Mrs. Baker down.' The words spilled honestly from Jennifer's mouth, an internal wince squeezed just as authentically.

'Mrs. Half-baked more like,' Peter said. 'The old bag can hardly walk, can hardly think; let's just tell her we're done, take the cash and blow this pop stand.'

That's not fair! echoed in Jennifer's mind, she clenched her fists three times — *Ignore it. Ignore It. Ignore it.*

She didn't have to say anything; they saw the words in her mind splash on her face. Jesus, why were they stuck here with the little ass-kisser on a Saturday afternoon? An idea struck Peter, charged his bones with childish meanness like a lightning bolt. It infected Sarah, a devilish flair making her eyes ignite and her lips gasp; she knew what he was thinking, the meanness becoming an infection.

'Well, okay, we'll stay,' Peter smiled, trying to hide the grin that ate away behind his lips, 'but you have to help us with something 'round the corner.'

'Sure,' Jennifer said.

The quickest of looks shared by Peter and Sarah, a spark of their individual meanness arced and conjoined. They moved behind the huge stacks of symmetrically stacked newspapers, printed columns that seemed to hold the shack's roof up. There, in-between them, near the back, stood an old rusted red locker. A tall, six-foot structure that needed to be put back into the ground with the amount of corrosion that ate away at it.

'That thing, we were going to clean that out. Wanna help?' Peter said.

She knew she didn't trust them, could feel herself not trusting them as they led her, grinning, towards the locker; but she still walked forward, didn't engage with her better judgment, common sense displaced for an empty autopilot.

'It's pretty ganky,' said Sarah, nothing genuine about her tone.

'Yeah take a look,' Peter said, and before she could think, before she could react, before she could clench her fists three times, before those words echoed in her mind — *Ignore it. Ignore It. Ignore it.*

Peter pushed Jennifer forward as the locker's door was yanked back by Sarah; she hurtled inside, head slamming straight into its back, the door quickly shoved shut by them both. Then complete darkness, then echoing whimpers not manifesting in her mind, but exiting her lips.

'How'd you like that, ginger freak!' Sarah laughed, Peter locking the door from the other side.

'Hey!' Jennifer called, banging on the cold steel door, throat immediately feeling as restricted as the rest of her body in the tight space.

'Please!' she pleaded, balled fists banging the door, the reverberating sounds of her pounding filling her ears.

'I wouldn't do that,' Peter said, 'it's not like you're in there… *alone.*'

'What do yo—' Jennifer blurted.

'Look up!' Sarah giggled.

Jennifer did, eyes wide and readjusting like the lenses of a movie camera. There was nothing, just cold endless darkness, just that moldy smell intensified, just…

Then she saw it. The thickest, grimmest cacophony of spider webbing she had ever seen, like a still haze of fog, or an ethereal mist frozen in time. It was a disgusting blanket of spinneret secretion that with each knock of her hands began to quiver, and at its edges, long thin hairy legs began to protrude from the sickening edge of darkness.

'Got some new friends in there, *Jennifer Blu*?' Sarah laughed.

'Please,' Jennifer whispered, shrinking down to the floor as far as possible, watching as above, the webbing bowed pregnantly, dipping as its silky mass was weighed down by the biggest spiders Jennifer had ever seen started to fill its space.

Little taps rattled out on the other side of the locker, both Peter and Sarah singing in rhythmic child's rhyme as they pattered their fingers against the cold metal.

'Night Creepers — Night Creepers, creeping up your nose, wriggling through your body; wriggling to your toes!'

A scared seriousness whistled past Jennifer's teeth, *'Please, let me out!'* each of the arachnid's eight eyes seemed to shine with a deep black opal desire, seemed to stare straight into her as she stared back.

'Pleaseeeee!' she whined.

They didn't stop.

'Night Creepers — Night Creepers, creeping through your hair, are running down your body, running everywhere!'

From above, eight legged bodies began to descend, opened wide like reaching claws; legs spread as if to smother their prey, ready to catch the girl who had entered their domain. It was like a bad dream, a vile nightmare that had bled to life.

'Night Creepers — Night Creepers, used to be a pest, now they're always with you, because you are their nest!'

'Have fun, *loser!*' Peter called, the pair laughing, running for the shed's door, leaving her locked in the locker.

Locked in the locker! Locked in darkness. Locked with the — *'Night Creepers — Night Creepers.'* Where did they learn that awful song? Why was this happening? The spiders knew someone was there; they were only coming out to greet her — all marble eyes, all spindly legs, all furry bodied. They lowered themselves on their webs past the locker's small vents where slats of sunlight beamed through; it cast ghastly shadows of the beasts.

Eight spiders were coming down, growing bigger as they descended towards her.

Tears began to bead from her eyes, skin itchy, goose bumps rising. She had hated spiders, insects and creepy crawly things — had they both known?

Night Creepers — Night Creepers.

It was an octagon of oversized arachnids, a mass of dangling legs coming down from each side.

She wanted to puke, wanted to vomit the fear that bred inside her, but didn't want to open her mouth, just in case — *Night Creepers — Night Creepers, creeping up your nose, wriggling through your body; wriggling to your toes!*

She tried to fiddle with the inside of the lock, could see its mechanism scraping up; if only she had something — anything to give it that extra leverage to slide between door and jamb, to pop it up, to pop it open.

She would do anything — *anything!*

'Please, help me!' she bawled, waiting for the inevitable, waiting for the eight-legged beasts to be on her. She put her hand to the floor of the locker, expecting more of the same, more awful insect life to touch her back. But there, beneath her right hand was what felt like a rigid piece of card, something thin and flat — something... that could be used to open the lock!

She sprang to action, slipped it in the jamb; pushed up, pushed hard, a slight metallic click entering her ears, a squirt of light feeling around the door as it creaked ajar.

Falling forward, falling free, she had escaped! Rubbing her hair, looking at her hands, expecting spiders — finding nothing. She looked over her shoulder, the locker door closing shut like a door to a mausoleum, an eerie whine commencing with its final click. The nightmare locked away inside, where it belonged.

She breathed out, shivered, sighed. looked down at what was in her hand — it was a card, not a playing card, what looked like a tarot card; old and worn. A grinning face stared from it: a red face, slicked black hair, thin moustache; pointed eyebrows that matched the horns protruding from his head. It was dead center in the card, one eye winking, the other seemingly staring straight at her. She knew the face, somehow knew all the names that went with it: Old scratch, Old gooseberry, Old thorn, Beelzebub,

Mephistopheles — The Devil. Underneath his grinning face, a slogan written on a curling scroll: "Come on Down!"

A wind seemed to find its way into the old shed, seemed to flitter the card, folding it, making it look like... The devil was winking... at her. And as he did, Jennifer Blu whispered the only thing she could, *'Thank you.'*

In her head, a reply echoed out in a voice that wasn't her own, *'No problem.'*

The mysterious wind blew again, a sulphurous smell tainting it: the wink returned.

She was away from the descending arachnids, free from the confines of the locker, and in a way, she owed him one, in a way she had made a deal. In a way he had saved her, and one day... she would have to repay the favor.

Coming Soon From David Irons

DON'T GO TO WHEELCHAIR CAMP

After a horrible accident that kills her sister, ten-year-old Terri Wilcox has to live her life in a wheelchair. She becomes a burden for her passive mom and aggressive dad. So one summer, they send Terri to Camp Cherry Plain – Wheelchair Camp. What no one knows is someone at Wheelchair Camp has a dark secret.

One by one, campers and counselors begin to die, and only a handful of the wheelchair-bound kids are left to fend for their lives as a brutal killer stalks them.

They should have been warned …

They should have been told …

Don't go to Wheelchair Camp.

It puts a new spin on terror.

 @severedpress
f /severedpress

SEVERED**PRESS**

Check out other great

Cryptid Novels!

Ian Faulkner

CRYPTID

Be careful what you look for. You might just find it.1996. A group of 14 students walked into the trackless virgin forests of Graham Island, British Columbia for a three-day hike. They were never seen again. 2019. An American TV crew retrace those students' steps to attempt to solve a 23-year-old mystery.A disparate collection of characters arrives on the island. But all is not as it seems. Two of them carry dark secrets. Terrible knowledge that will mean death for some – but a fighting chance of survival for others. In the hidden depths of the forests – man is on the menu. Some mysteries should remain unsolved...

Eric S. Brown

LOCH NESS HORROR

The Order of the Eternal Light, a secret organization have foretold the end of the human race. In order to save all humanity, agents of the Order must locate the Loch Ness Monster and obtain a sample of its blood for within in it is the key to stopping the apocalypse but finding the monster will be no easy task.

Check out other great

Cryptid Novels!

Hunter Shea

LOCH NESS REVENGE

Deep in the murky waters of Loch Ness, the creature known as Nessie has returned. Twins Natalie and Austin McQueen watched in horror as their parents were devoured by the world's most infamous lake monster. Two decades later, it's their turn to hunt the legend. But what lurks in the Loch is not what they expected. Nessie is devouring everything in and around the Loch, and it's not alone. Hell has come to the Scottish Highlands. In a fierce battle between man and monster, the world may never be the same. Praise for THEY RISE : "Outrageous, balls to the wall...made me yearn for 3D glasses and a tub of popcorn, extra butter!" – The Eyes of Madness "A fast-paced, gore-heavy splatter fest of sharksploitation." The Werd "A rocket paced horror story. I enjoyed the hell out of this book." Shotgun Logic Reviews

C.G. Mosley

BAKER COUNTY BIGFOOT CHRONICLE

Marie Bledsoe only wants her missing brother Kurt back. She'll stop at nothing to make it happen and, with the help of Kurt's friend Tony, along with Sheriff Ray Cochran, Marie embarks on a terrifying journey deep into the belly of the mysterious Walker Laboratory to find him. However, what she and her companions find lurking in the laboratory basement is beyond comprehension. There are cryptids from the forest being held captive there and something...else. Enjoy this suspenseful tale from the mind of C.G. Mosley, author of Wood Ape. Welcome back to Baker County, a place where monsters do lurk in the night!